MARTHA SPEAKS

CANINE COMICS

Adaptation by Jamie White
Based on TV series teleplays written by
Peter K. Hirsch
Ron Holsey
Maria Finn
Raye Lankford
Ken Scarborough
Matt Steinglass

Based on the characters created by Susan Meddaugh

Houghton Mifflin Harcourt
Boston • New York • 2012

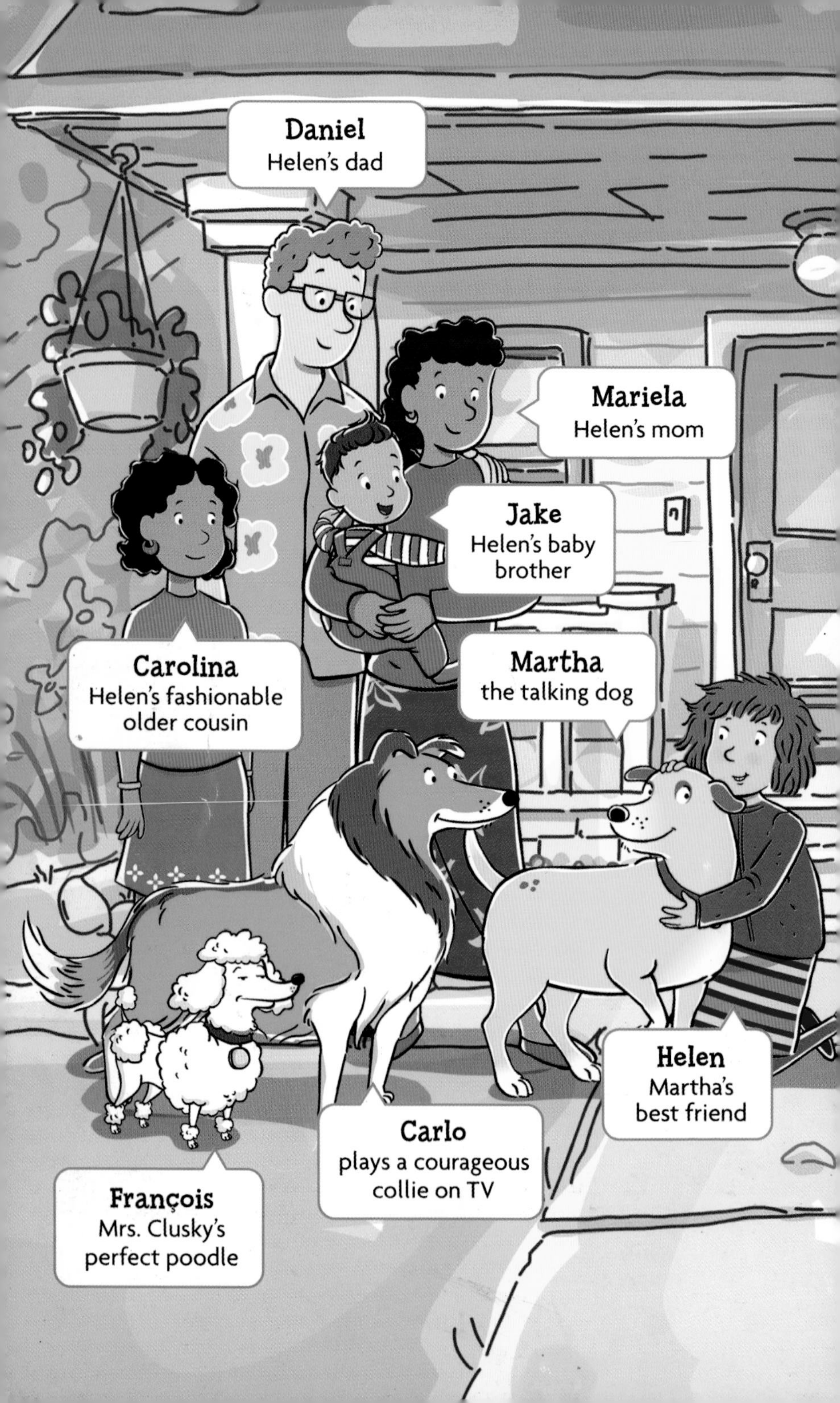
Daniel
Helen's dad
Mariela
Helen's mom
Jake
Helen's baby brother
Carolina
Helen's fashionable older cousin
Martha
the talking dog
Helen
Martha's best friend
Carlo
plays a courageous collie on TV
François
Mrs. Clusky's perfect poodle

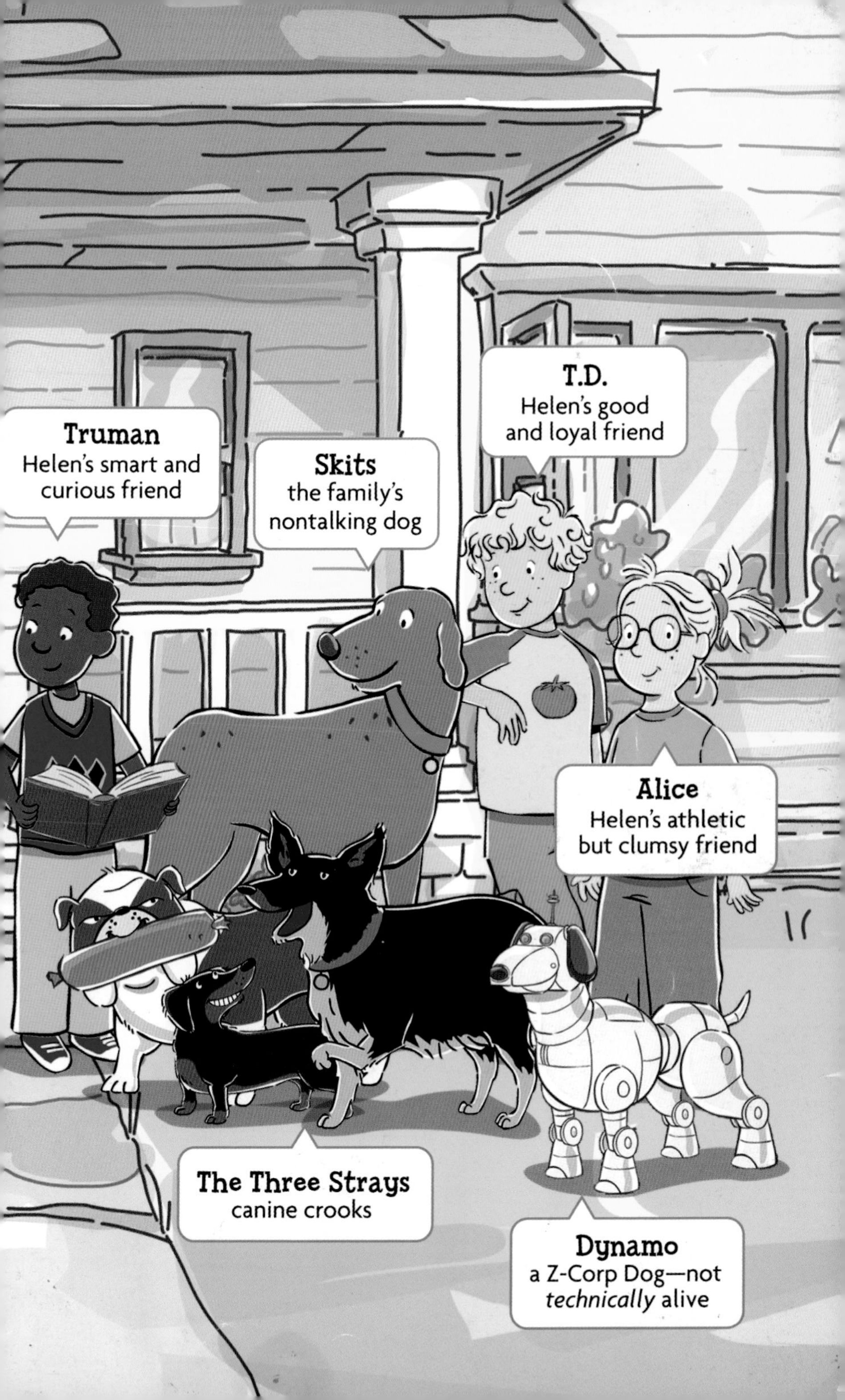

Truman
Helen's smart and curious friend
Skits
the family's nontalking dog
T.D.
Helen's good and loyal friend
Alice
Helen's athletic but clumsy friend
The Three Strays
canine crooks
Dynamo
a Z-Corp Dog—not *technically* alive

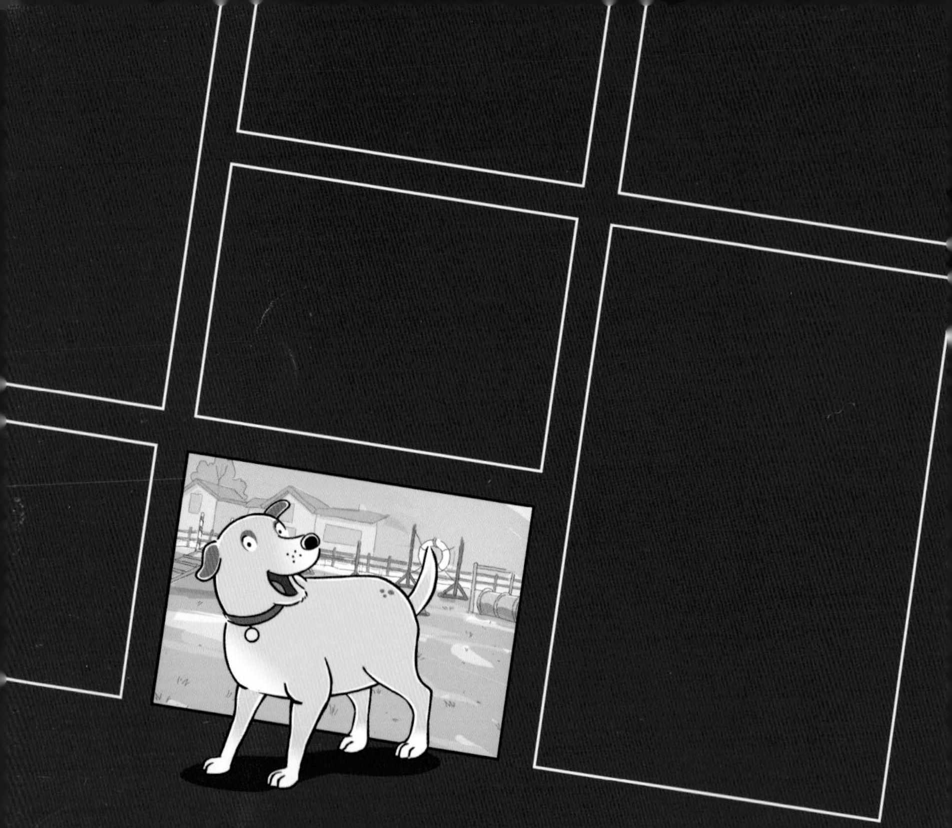

ISBN: 978-0-547-86784-7

Cover design by Rachel Newborn
Book design by Bill Smith Studio

www.hmhbooks.com
www.marthathetalkingdog.com

Manufactured in China
SCP 10 9 8 7 6 5 4 3 2 1
4500384903

SIX UNBELIEVABLE COMICS!

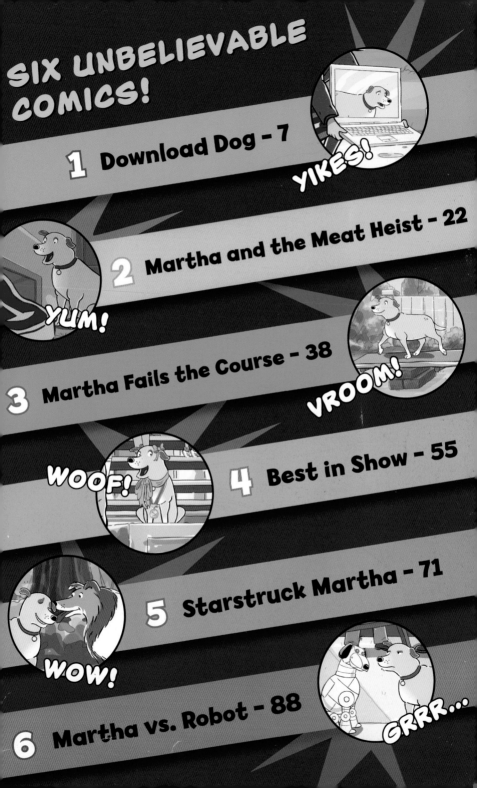

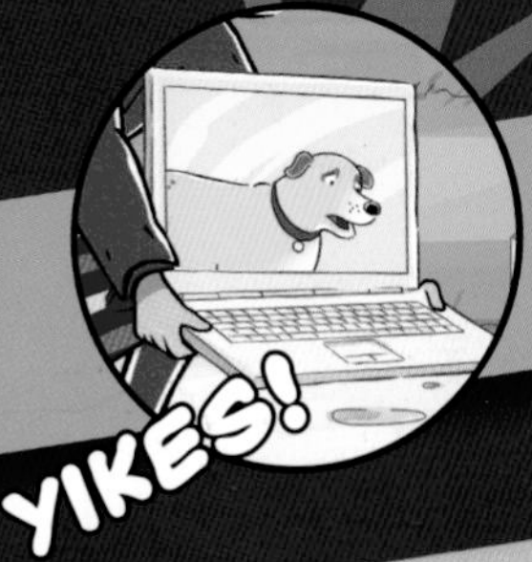
YIKES!

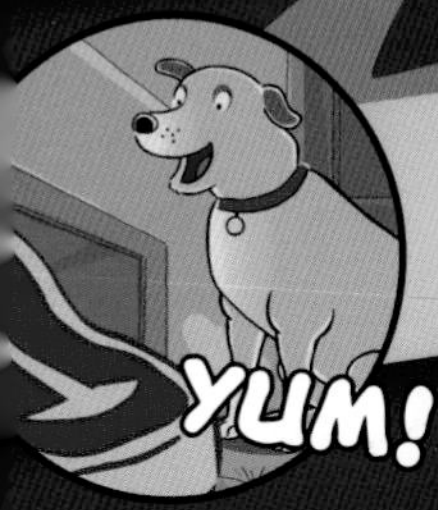
YUM!

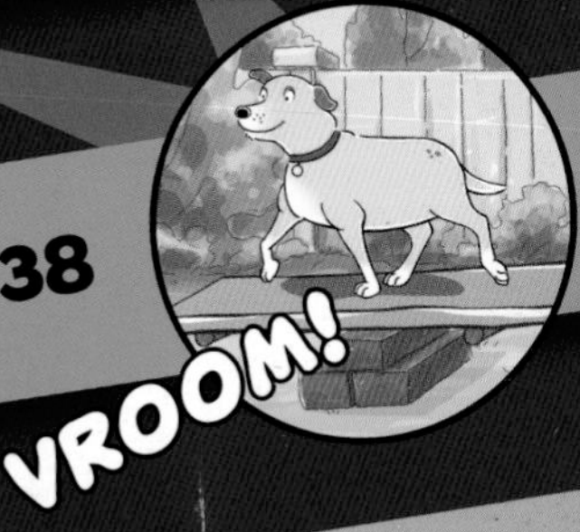
VROOM!

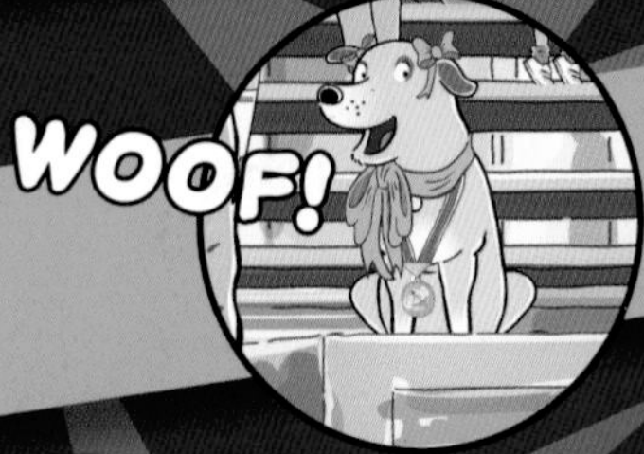
WOOF!

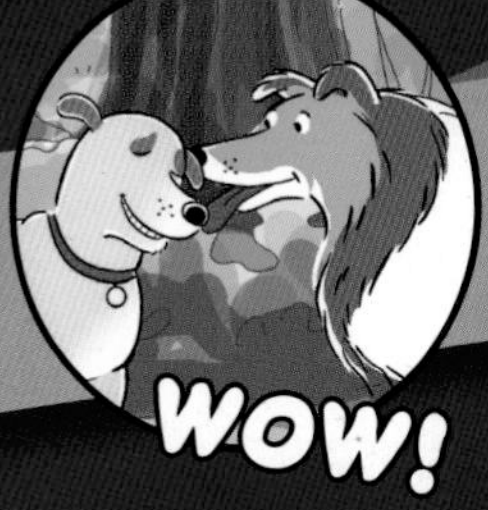
WOW!

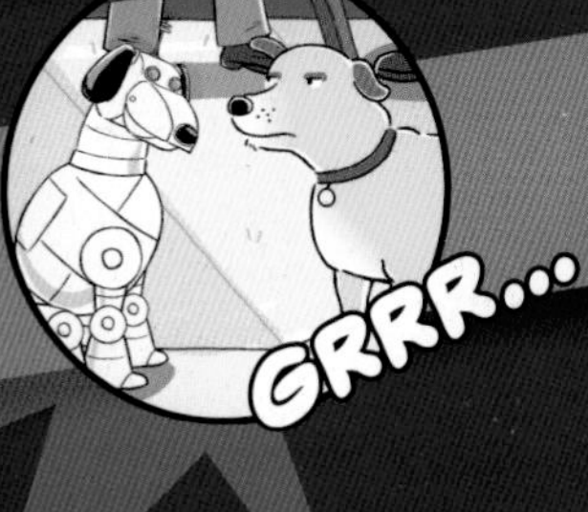
GRRR...

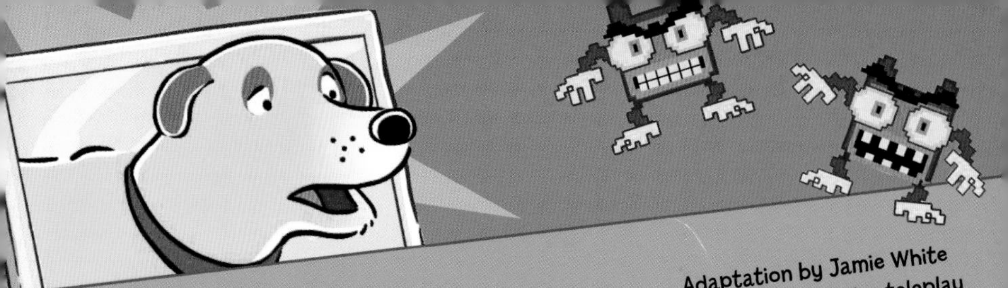

1 Download Dog

Adaptation by Jamie White
Based on a TV series teleplay
written by Ken Scarborough

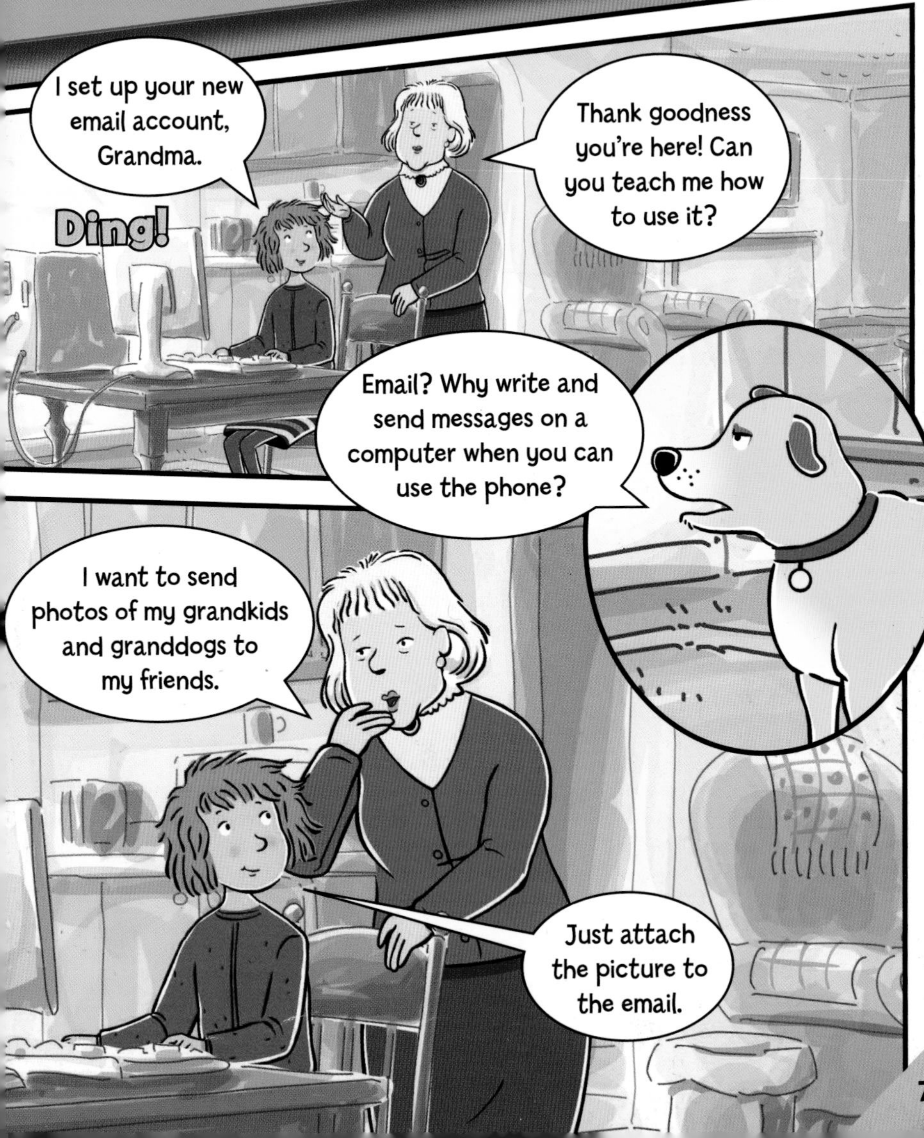
I set up your new email account, Grandma.
Ding!
Thank goodness you're here! Can you teach me how to use it?
Email? Why write and send messages on a computer when you can use the phone?
I want to send photos of my grandkids and granddogs to my friends.
Just attach the picture to the email.

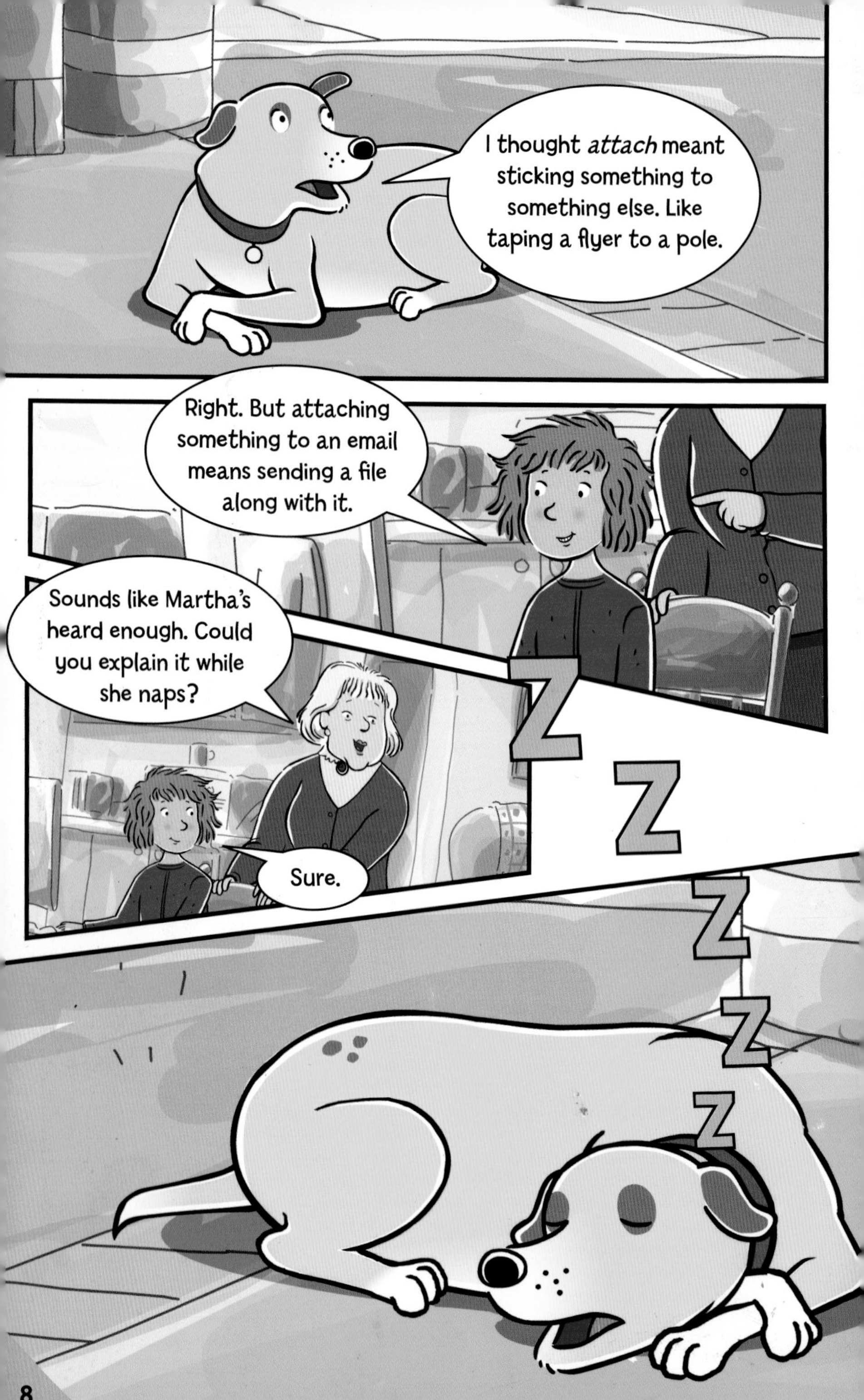
I thought *attach* meant sticking something to something else. Like taping a flyer to a pole.
Right. But attaching something to an email means sending a file along with it.
Sounds like Martha's heard enough. Could you explain it while she naps?
Sure.
Z Z Z Z Z

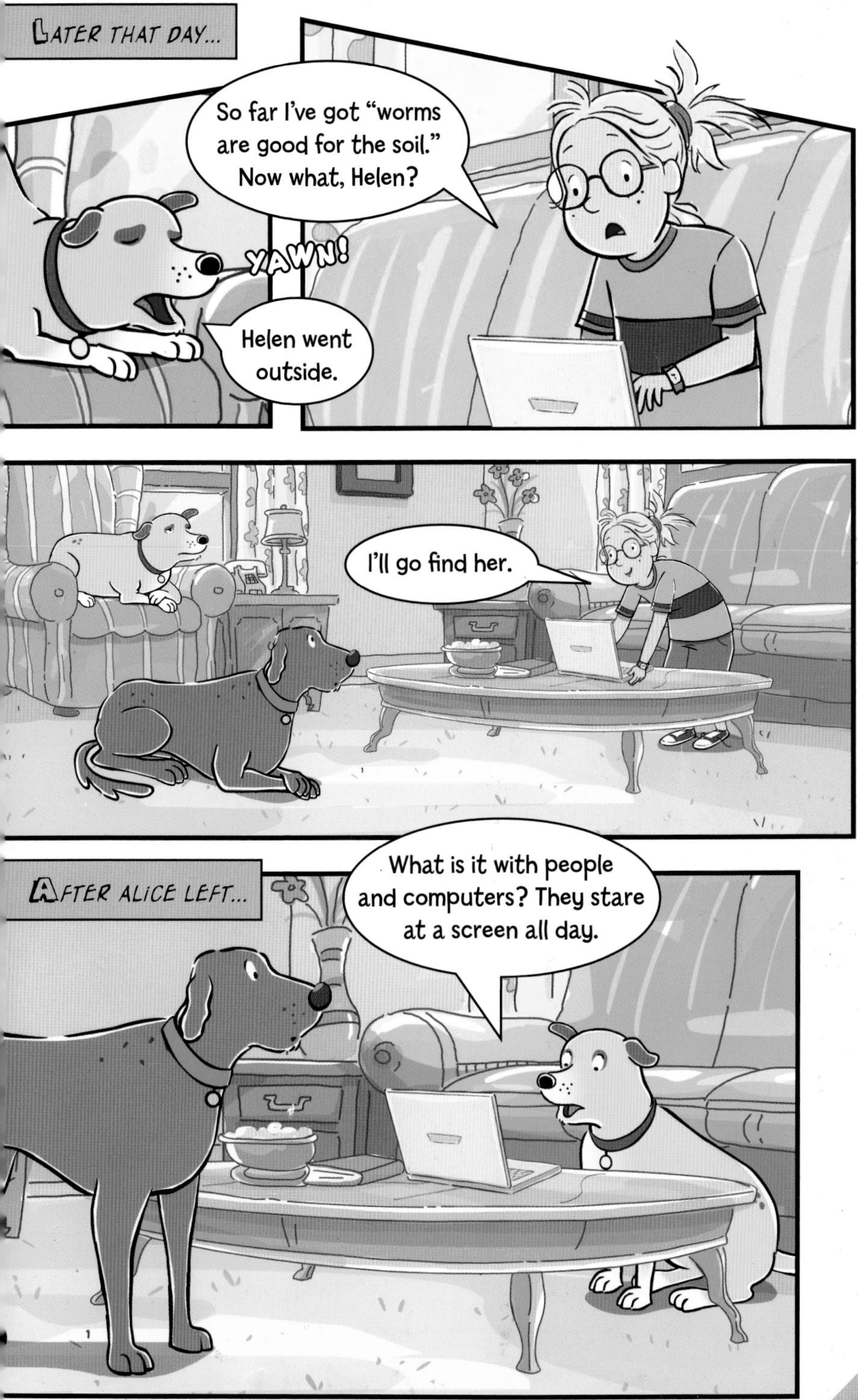
LATER THAT DAY...
So far I've got "worms are good for the soil." Now what, Helen?
YAWN!
Helen went outside.
I'll go find her.
AFTER ALICE LEFT...
What is it with people and computers? They stare at a screen all day.

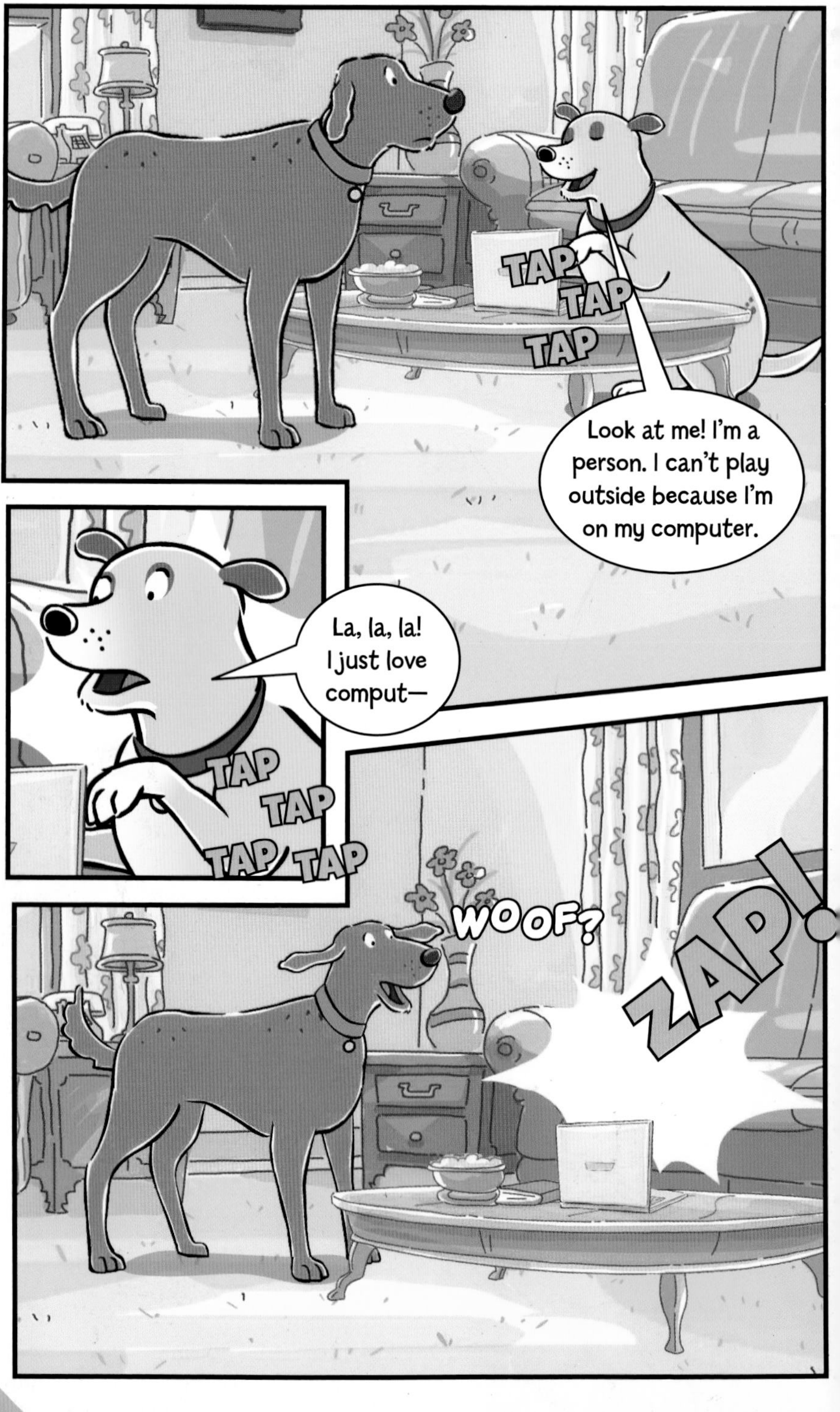
TAP
TAP
TAP
Look at me! I'm a person. I can't play outside because I'm on my computer.
La, la, la! I just love comput—
TAP
TAP
TAP
TAP
WOOF?
ZAP!

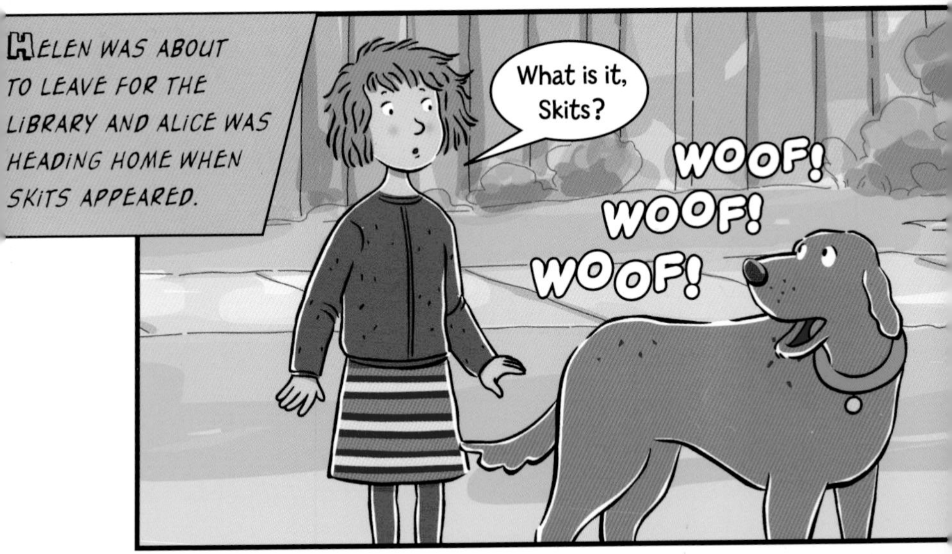
HELEN WAS ABOUT TO LEAVE FOR THE LIBRARY AND ALICE WAS HEADING HOME WHEN SKITS APPEARED.
What is it, Skits?
WOOF!
WOOF!
WOOF!

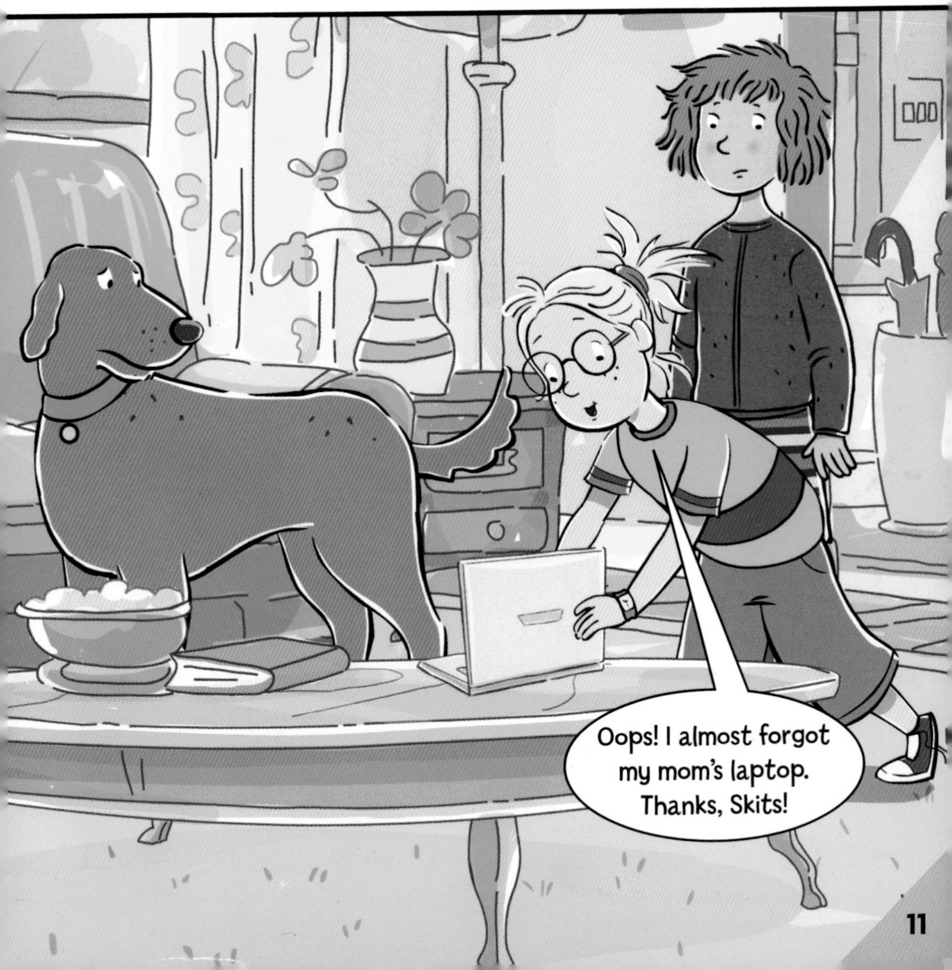
Oops! I almost forgot my mom's laptop. Thanks, Skits!

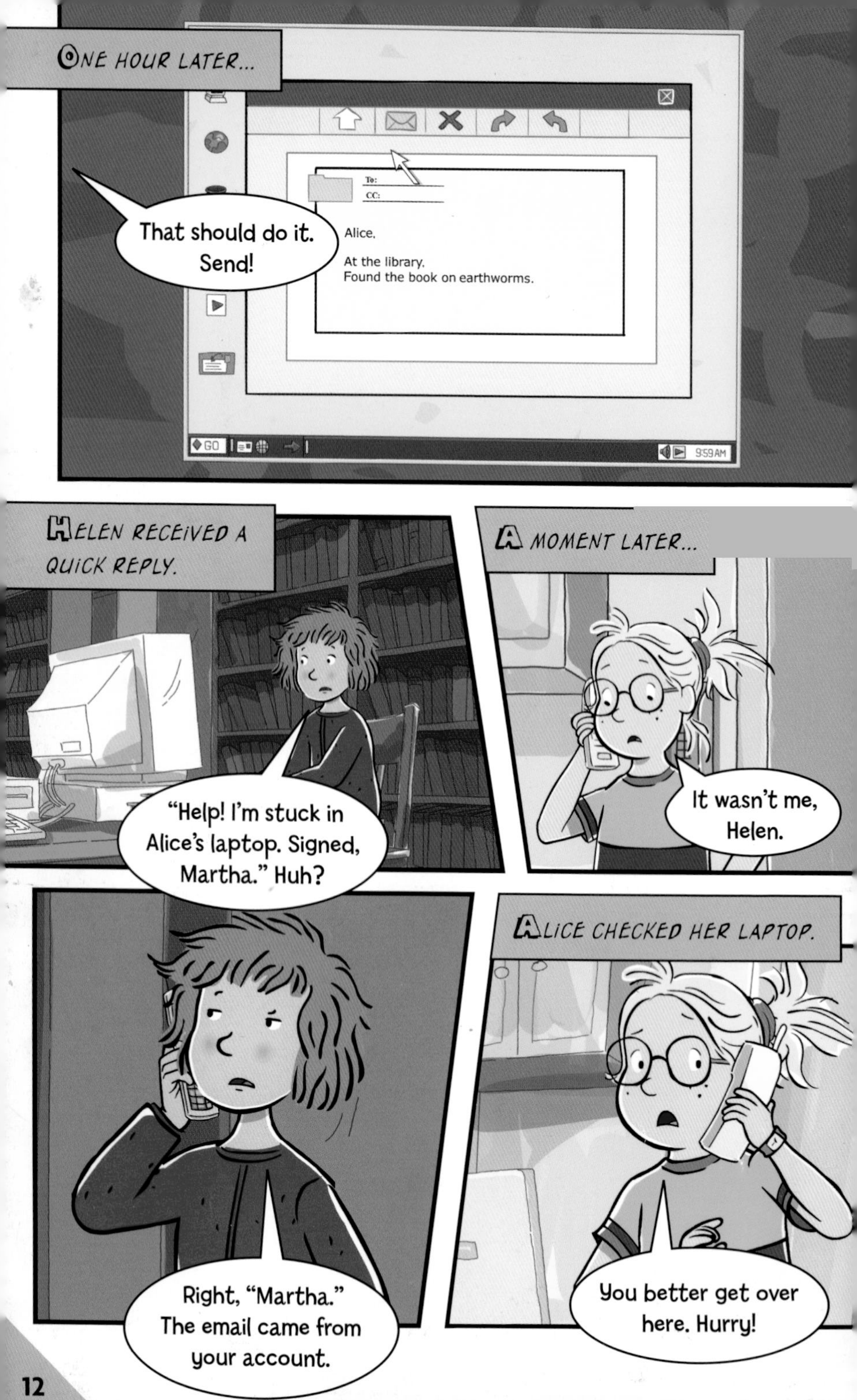
ONE HOUR LATER...
To:
CC:
Alice,
At the library,
Found the book on earthworms.
That should do it. Send!
GO
9:59 AM
HELEN RECEIVED A QUICK REPLY.
"Help! I'm stuck in Alice's laptop. Signed, Martha." Huh?
A MOMENT LATER...
It wasn't me, Helen.
Right, "Martha." The email came from your account.
ALICE CHECKED HER LAPTOP.
You better get over here. Hurry!

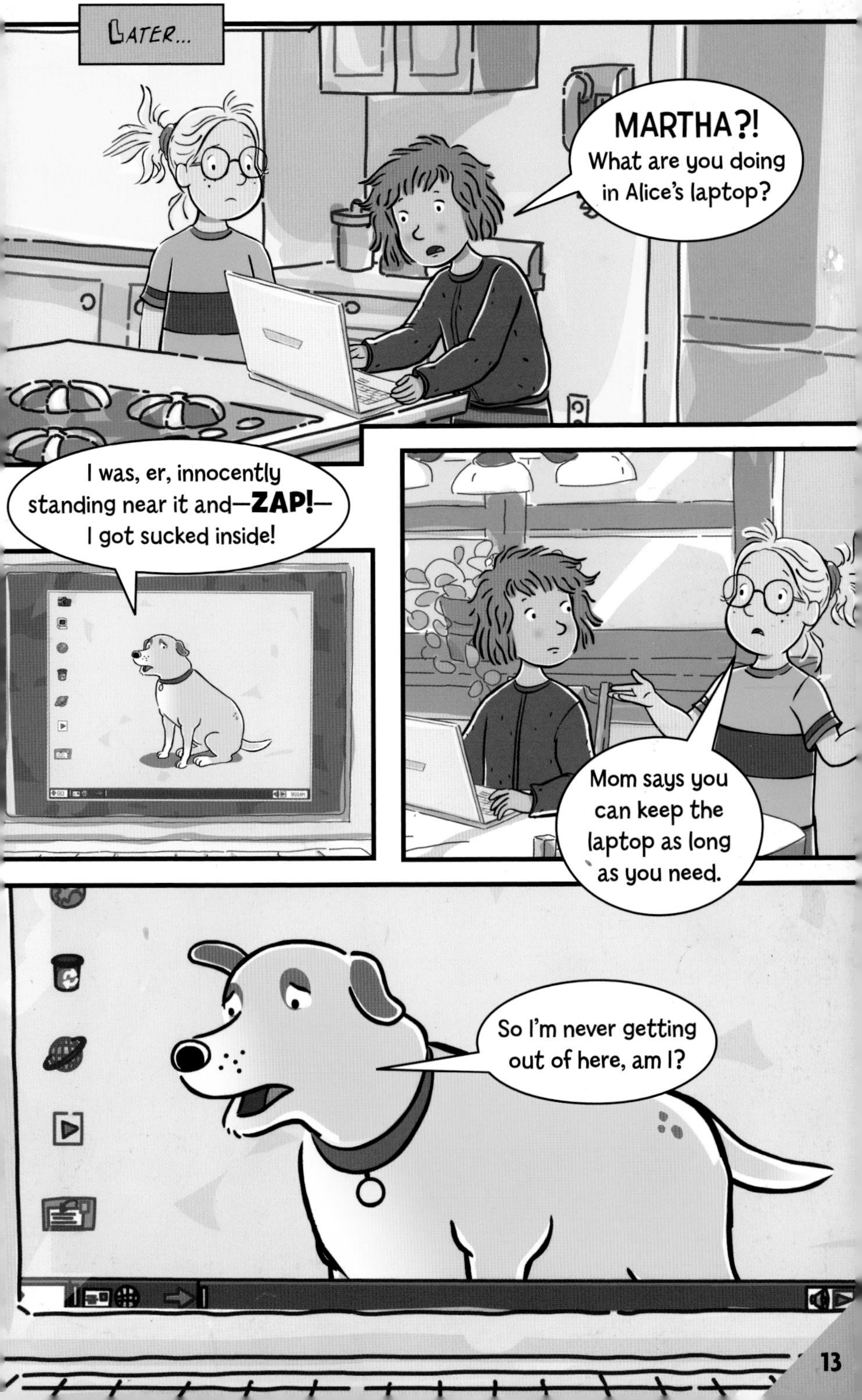
LATER...
MARTHA?! What are you doing in Alice's laptop?
I was, er, innocently standing near it and—ZAP!—I got sucked inside!
Mom says you can keep the laptop as long as you need.
So I'm never getting out of here, am I?

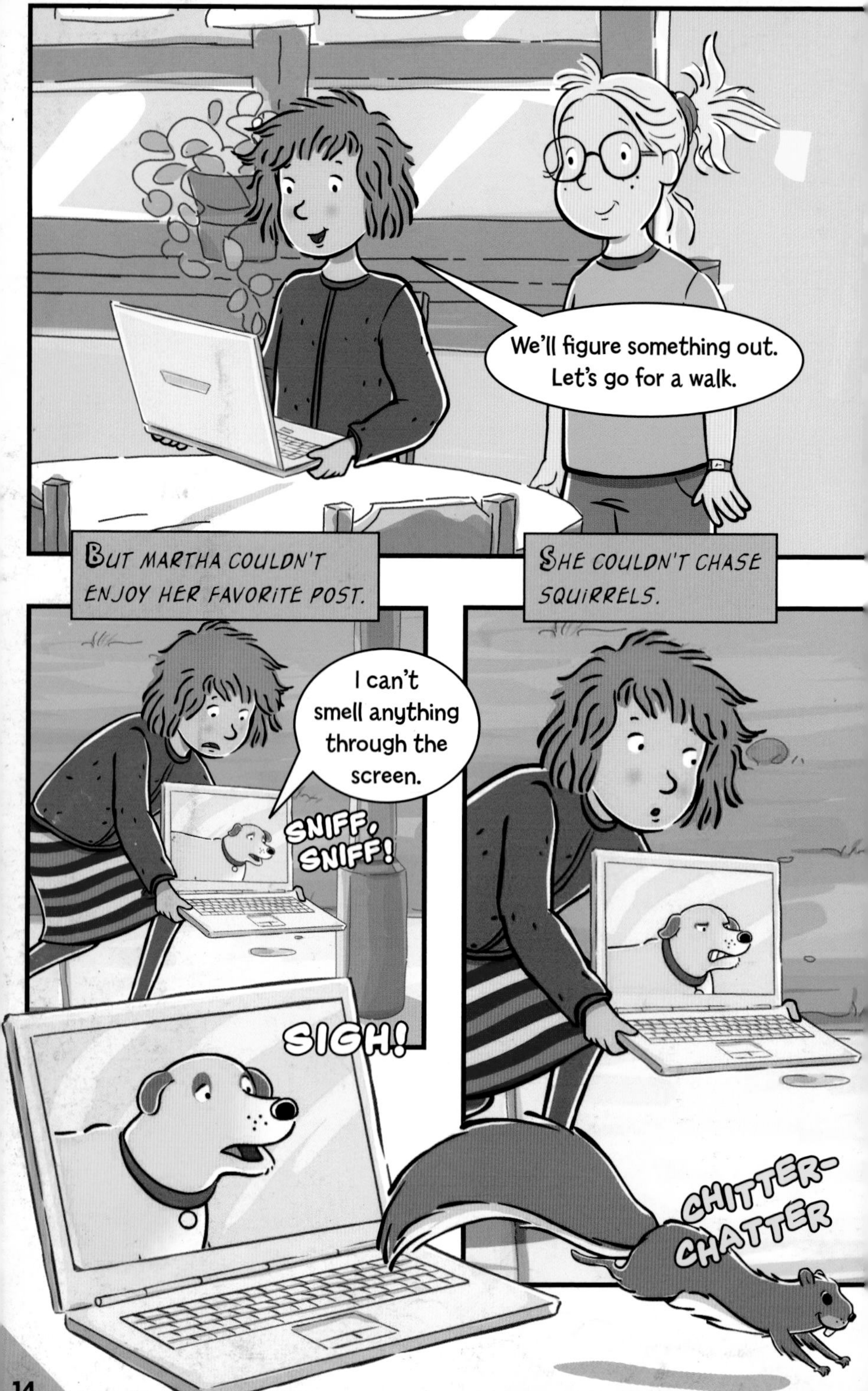
We'll figure something out. Let's go for a walk.
BUT MARTHA COULDN'T ENJOY HER FAVORITE POST.
I can't smell anything through the screen.
SNIFF, SNIFF!
SIGH!
SHE COULDN'T CHASE SQUIRRELS.
CHITTER-CHATTER

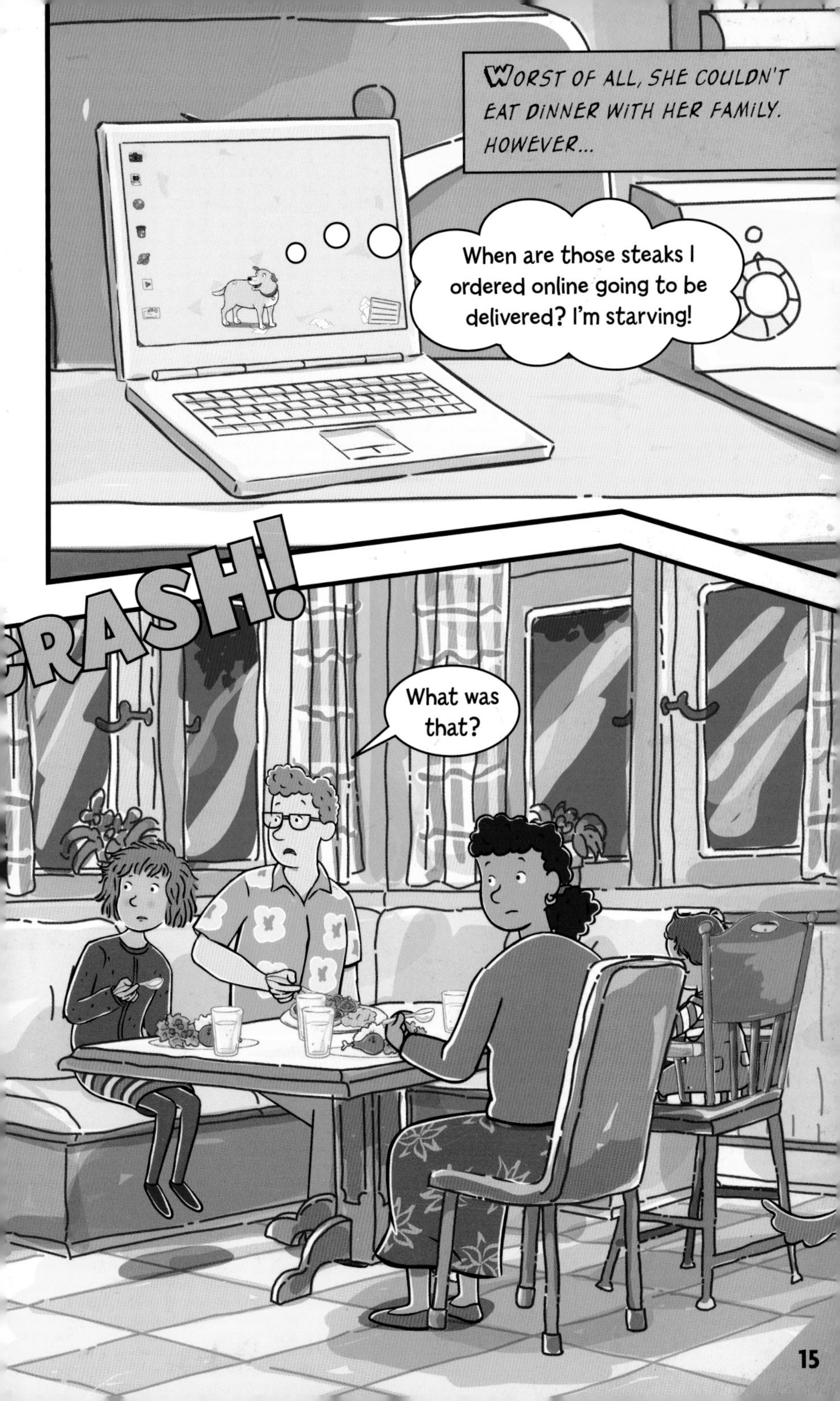
WORST OF ALL, SHE COULDN'T EAT DINNER WITH HER FAMILY. HOWEVER...
When are those steaks I ordered online going to be delivered? I'm starving!
CRASH!
What was that?

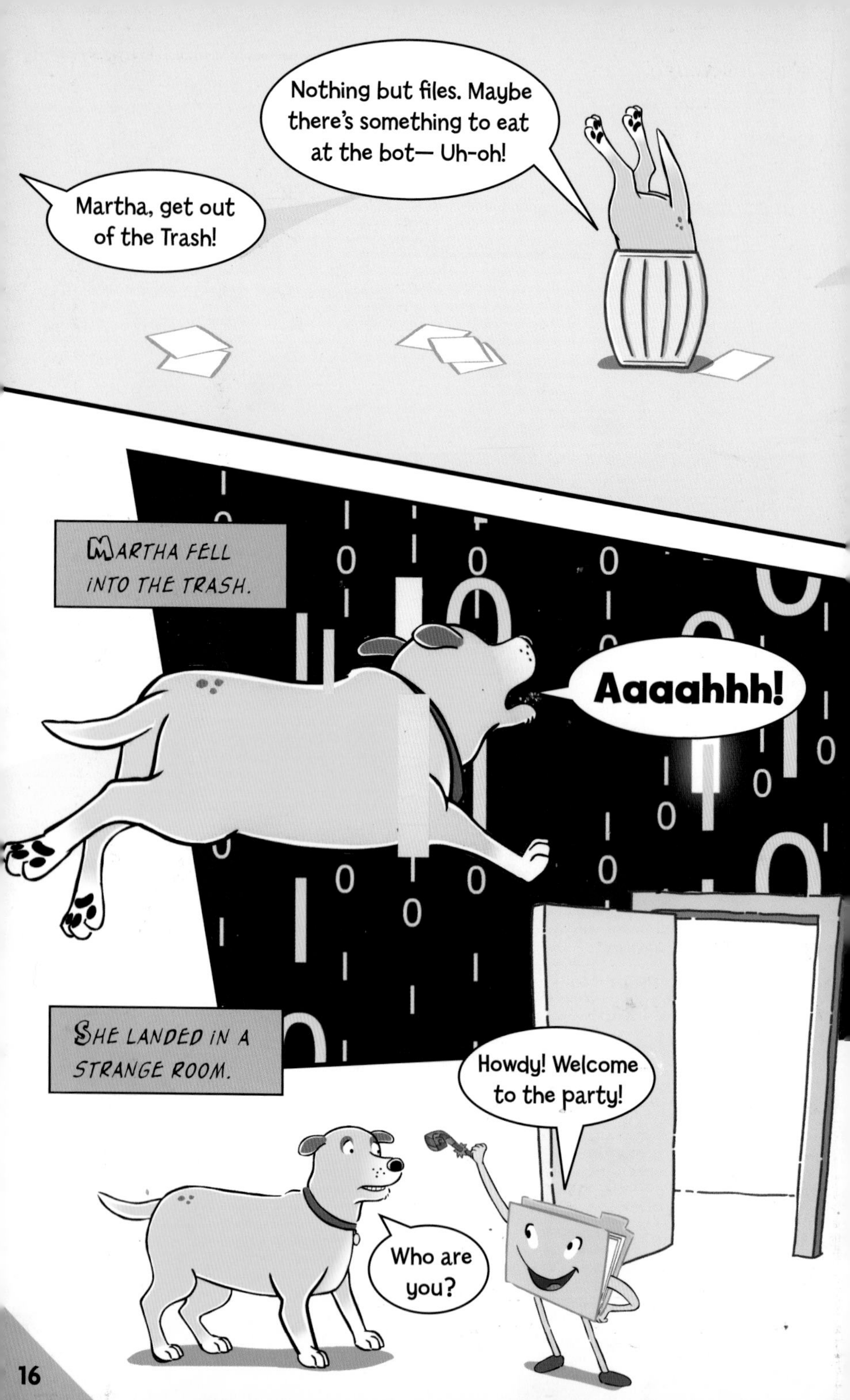
Martha, get out of the Trash!
Nothing but files. Maybe there's something to eat at the bot— Uh-oh!
MARTHA FELL INTO THE TRASH.
Aaaahhh!
SHE LANDED IN A STRANGE ROOM.
Howdy! Welcome to the party!
Who are you?

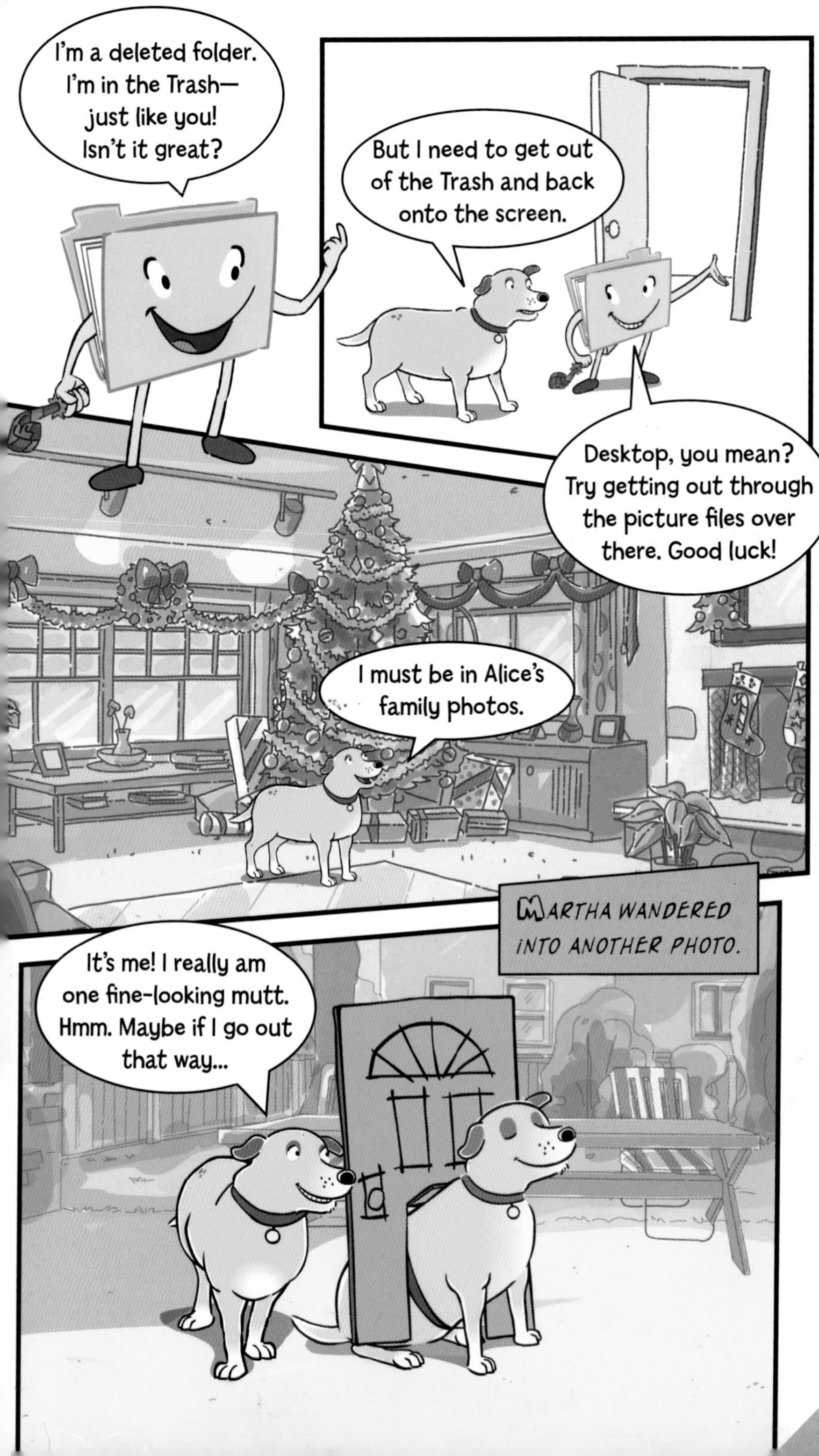
I'm a deleted folder. I'm in the Trash—just like you! Isn't it great?
But I need to get out of the Trash and back onto the screen.
Desktop, you mean? Try getting out through the picture files over there. Good luck!
I must be in Alice's family photos.
MARTHA WANDERED INTO ANOTHER PHOTO.
It's me! I really am one fine-looking mutt. Hmm. Maybe if I go out that way...

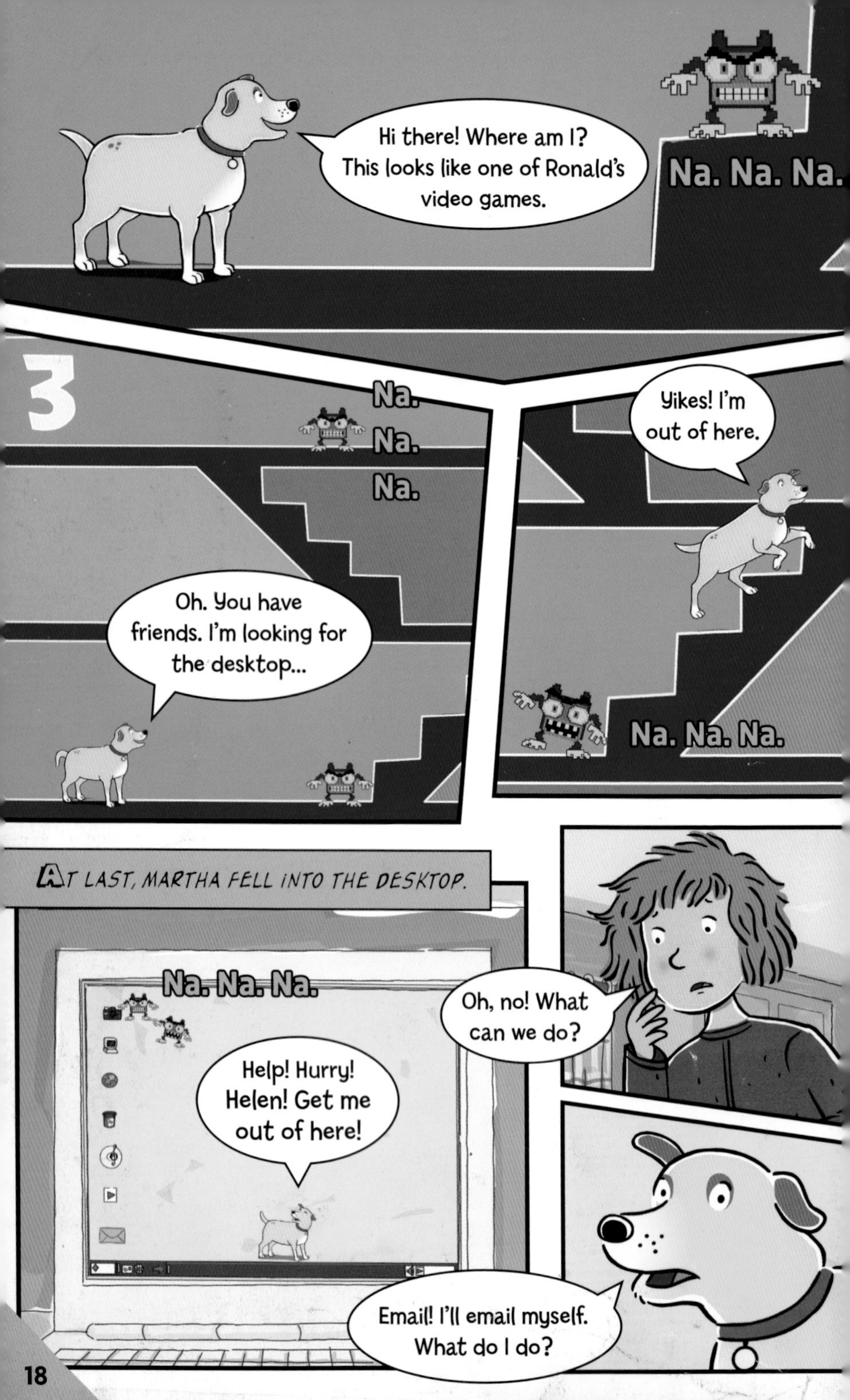
Hi there! Where am I? This looks like one of Ronald's video games.
Na. Na. Na.
3
Na.
Na.
Na.
Oh. You have friends. I'm looking for the desktop...
Yikes! I'm out of here.
Na. Na. Na.
AT LAST, MARTHA FELL INTO THE DESKTOP.
Na. Na. Na.
Help! Hurry! Helen! Get me out of here!
Oh, no! What can we do?
Email! I'll email myself. What do I do?

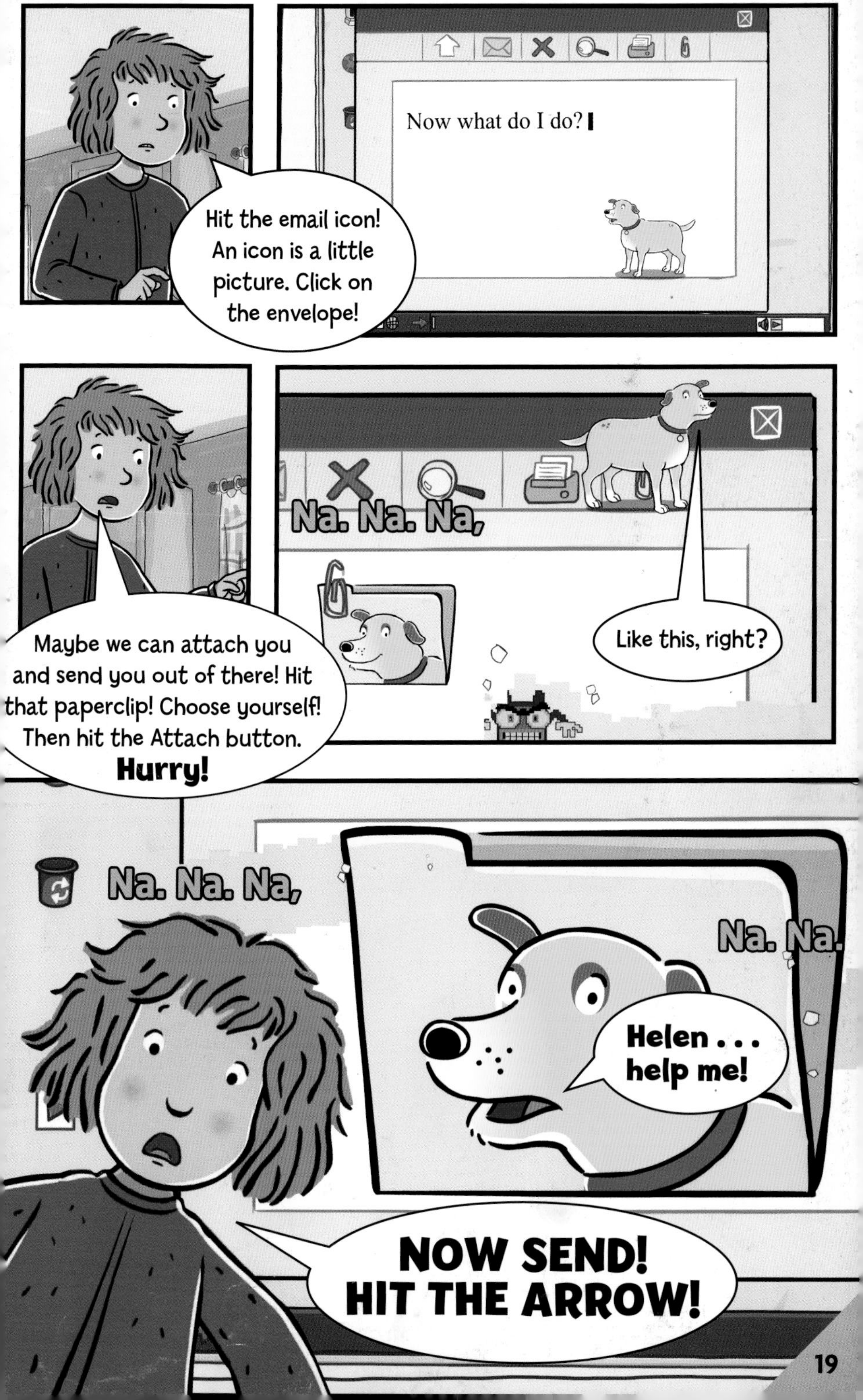

Now what do I do?
Hit the email icon! An icon is a little picture. Click on the envelope!
Na. Na. Na,
Maybe we can attach you and send you out of there! Hit that paperclip! Choose yourself! Then hit the Attach button. **Hurry!**
Like this, right?
Na. Na. Na,
Na. Na.
Helen . . . help me!
NOW SEND! HIT THE ARROW!

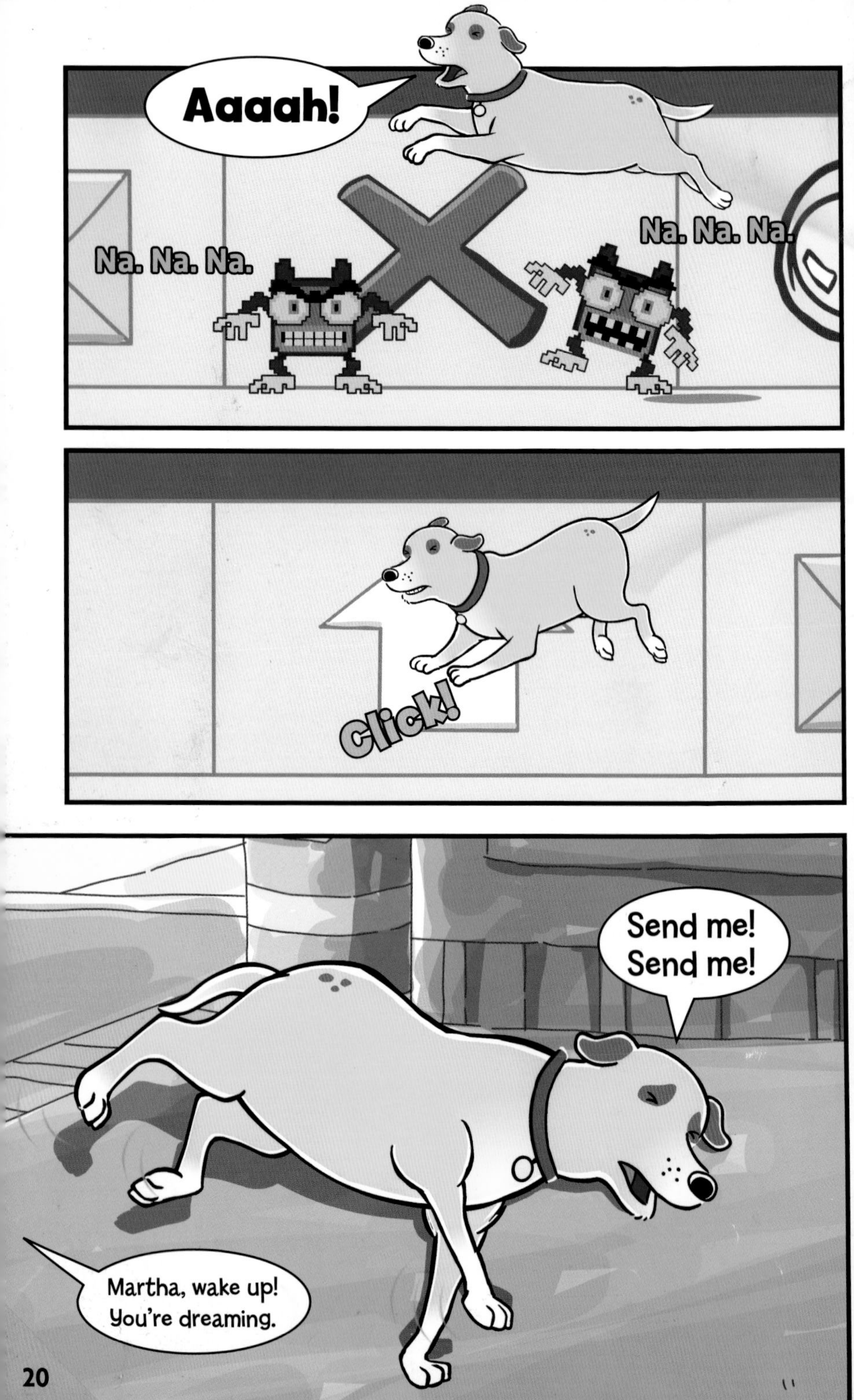
Aaaah!
Na. Na. Na.
Na. Na. Na.
Click!
Send me! Send me!
Martha, wake up! You're dreaming.

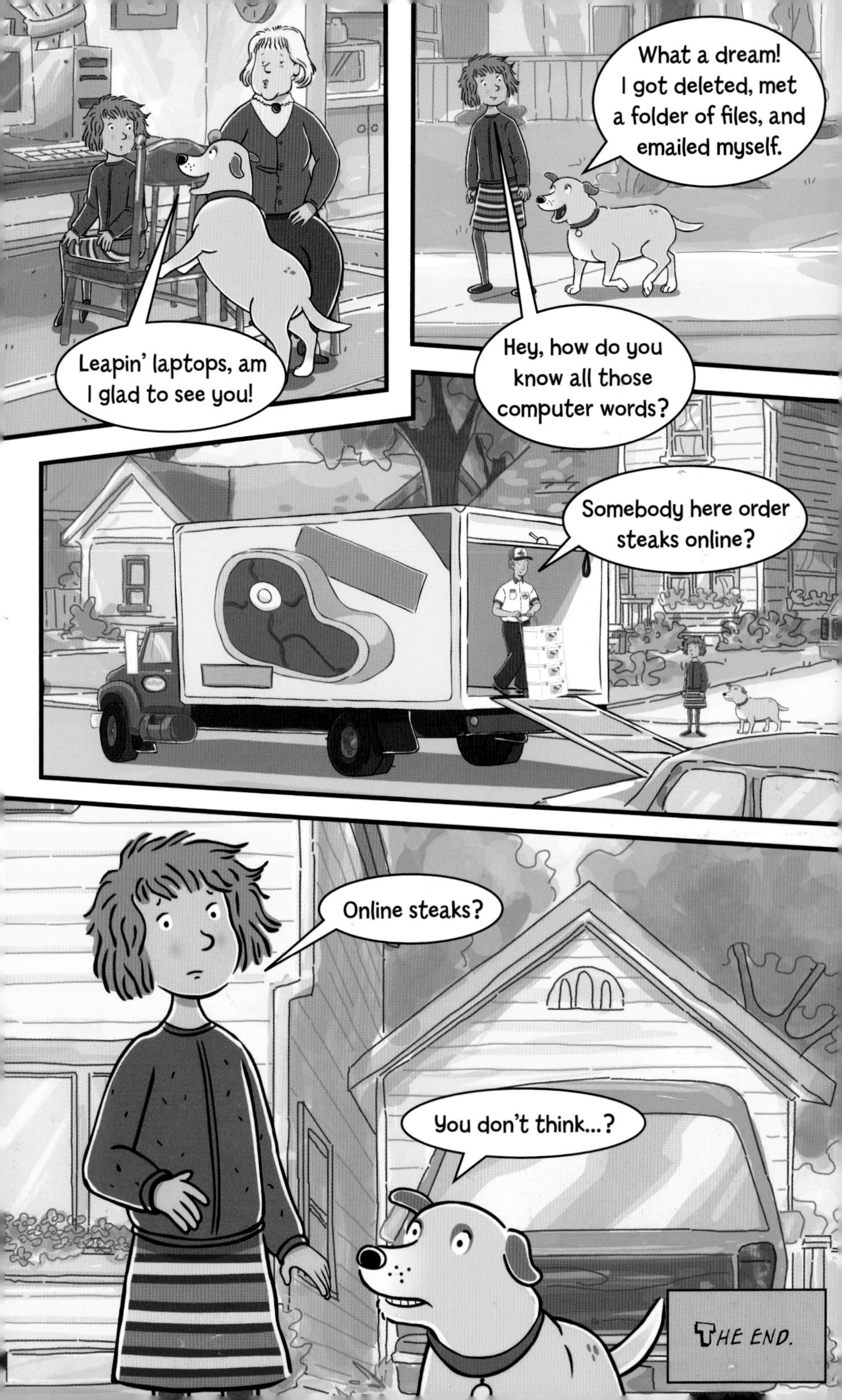
Leapin' laptops, am I glad to see you!
What a dream! I got deleted, met a folder of files, and emailed myself.
Hey, how do you know all those computer words?
Somebody here order steaks online?
Online steaks?
You don't think...?
THE END.

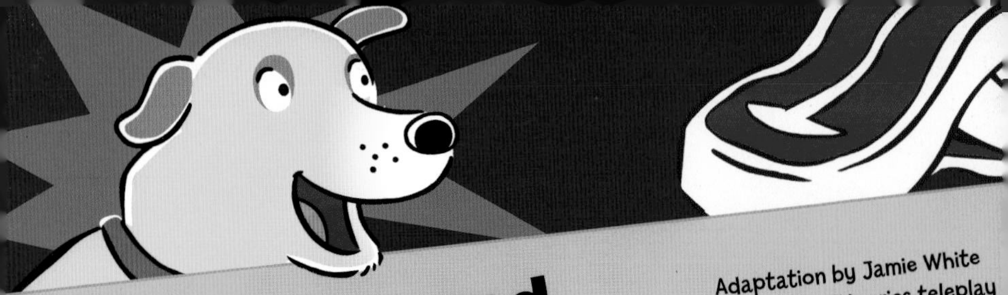

2 Martha and the Meat Heist

Adaptation by Jamie White
Based on a TV series teleplay
written by Peter K. Hirsch

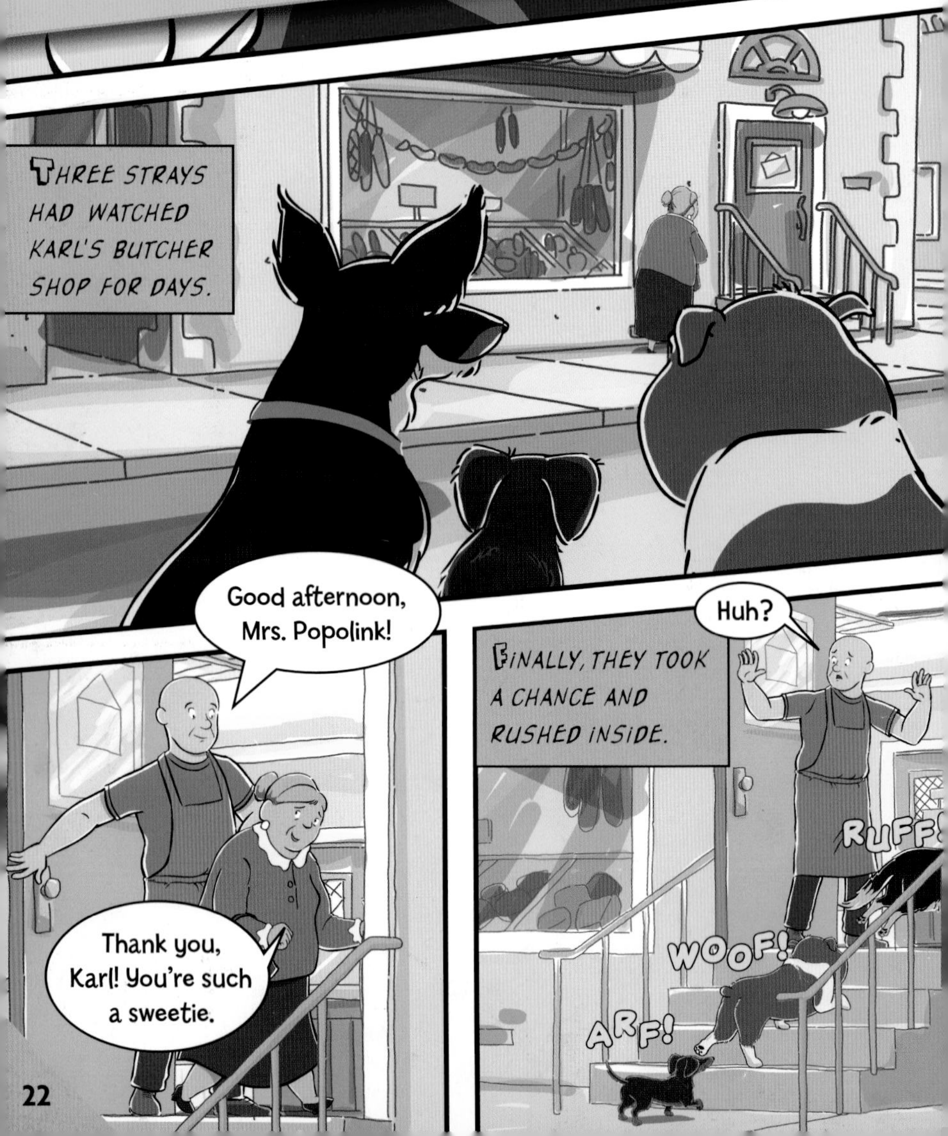

THREE STRAYS HAD WATCHED KARL'S BUTCHER SHOP FOR DAYS.
Good afternoon, Mrs. Popolink!
Thank you, Karl! You're such a sweetie.
Huh?
FINALLY, THEY TOOK A CHANCE AND RUSHED INSIDE.
RUFF
WOOF!
ARF!

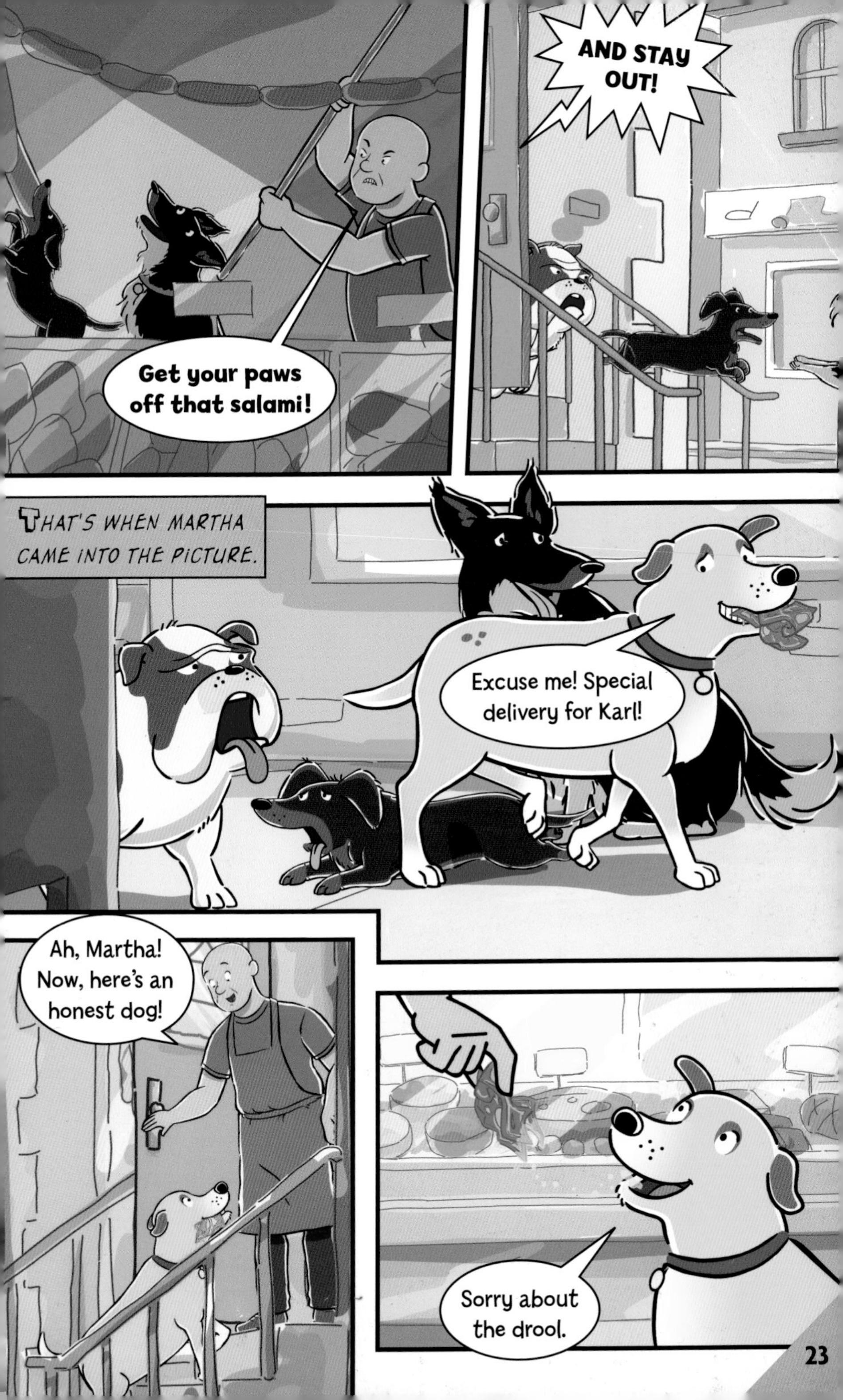
Get your paws off that salami!
AND STAY OUT!
THAT'S WHEN MARTHA CAME INTO THE PICTURE.
Excuse me! Special delivery for Karl!
Ah, Martha! Now, here's an honest dog!
Sorry about the drool.

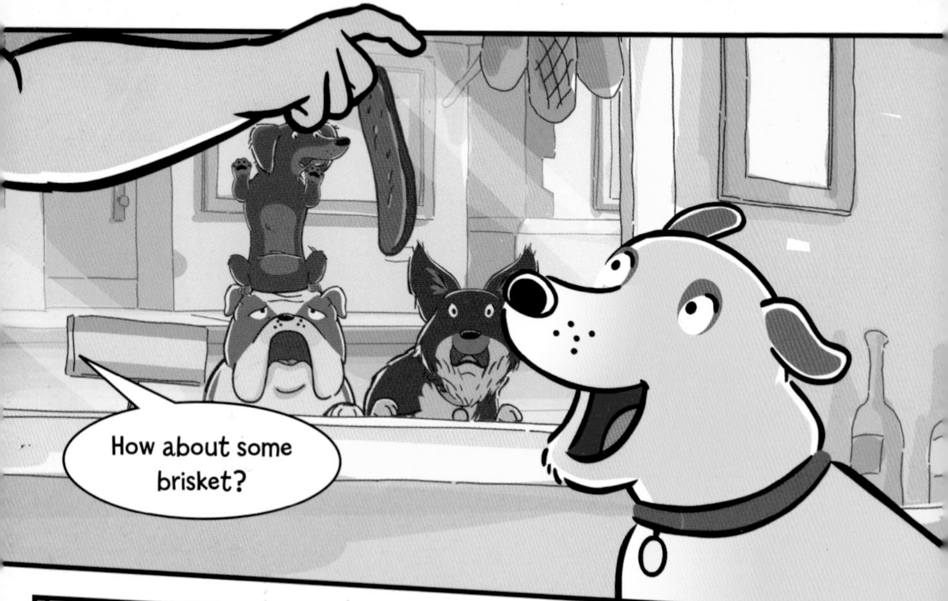
How about some brisket?

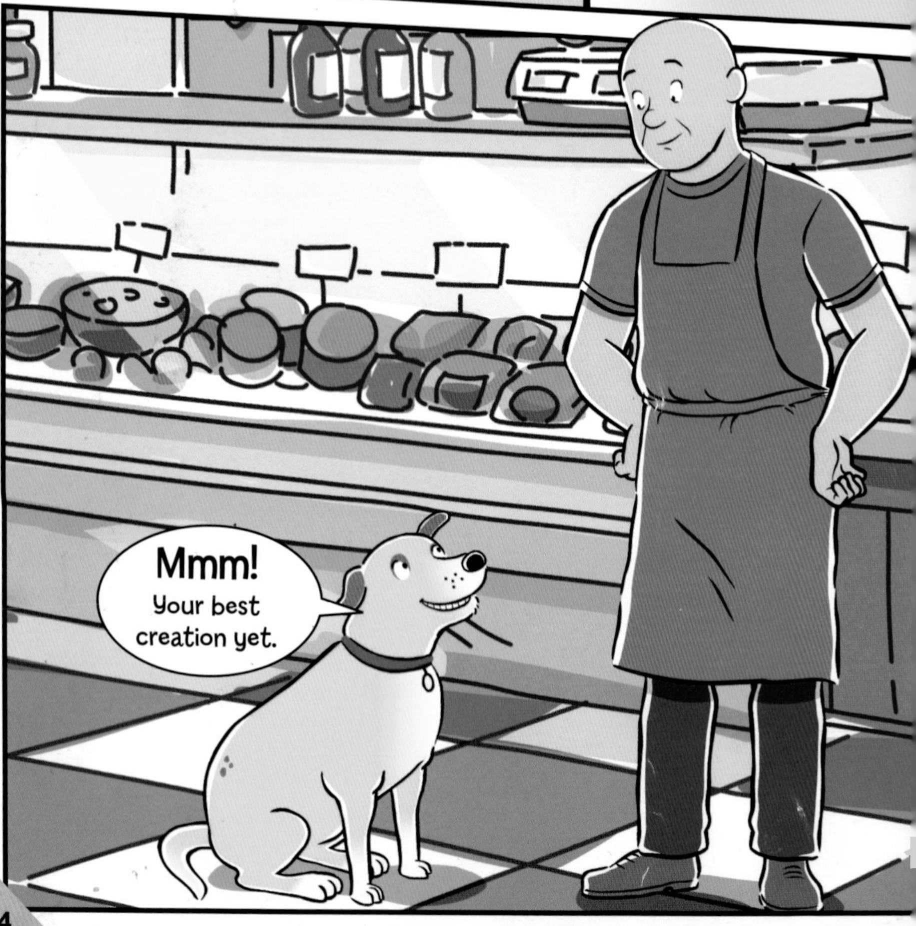
Mmm! Your best creation yet.

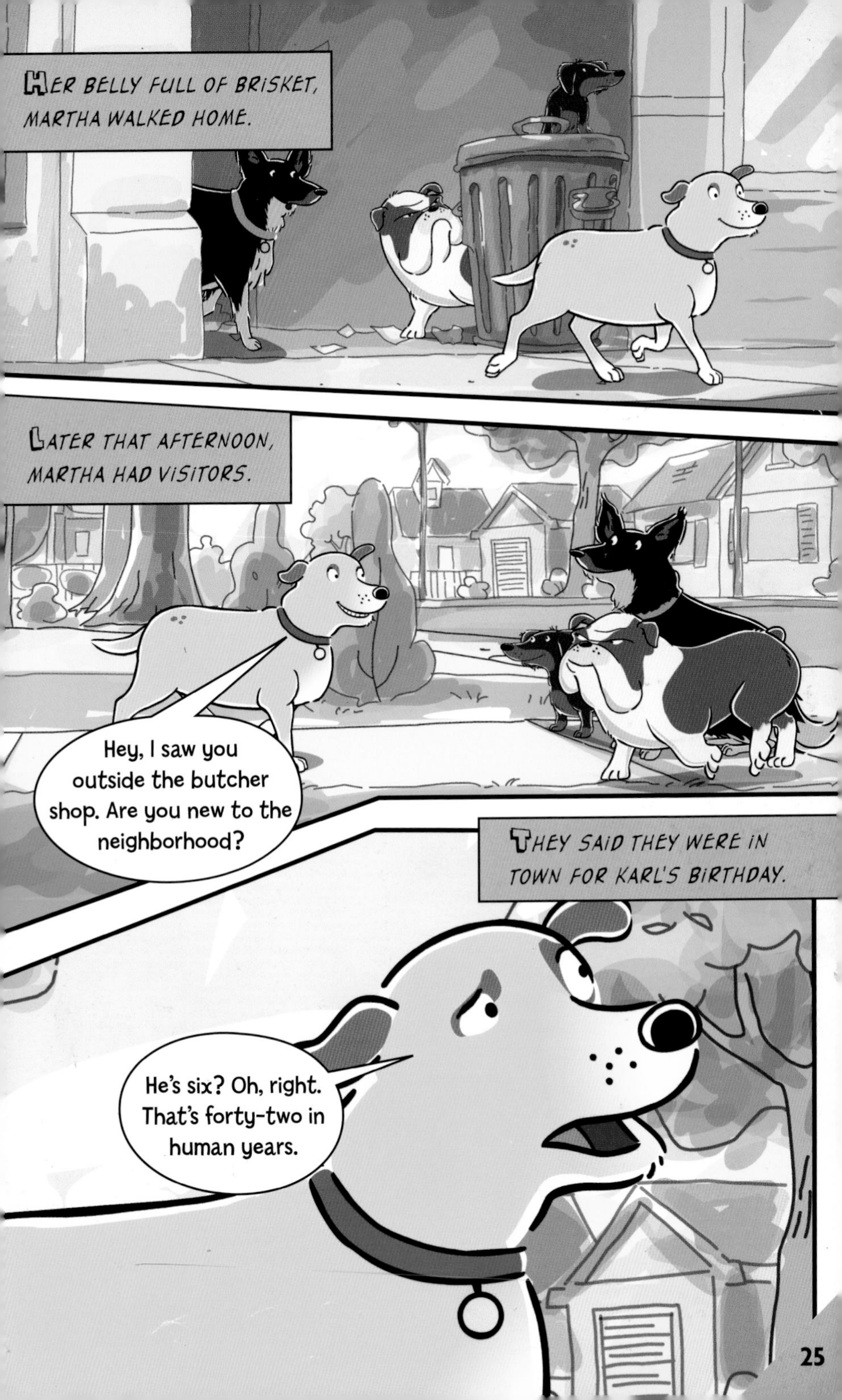
HER BELLY FULL OF BRISKET, MARTHA WALKED HOME.
LATER THAT AFTERNOON, MARTHA HAD VISITORS.
Hey, I saw you outside the butcher shop. Are you new to the neighborhood?
THEY SAID THEY WERE IN TOWN FOR KARL'S BIRTHDAY.
He's six? Oh, right. That's forty-two in human years.

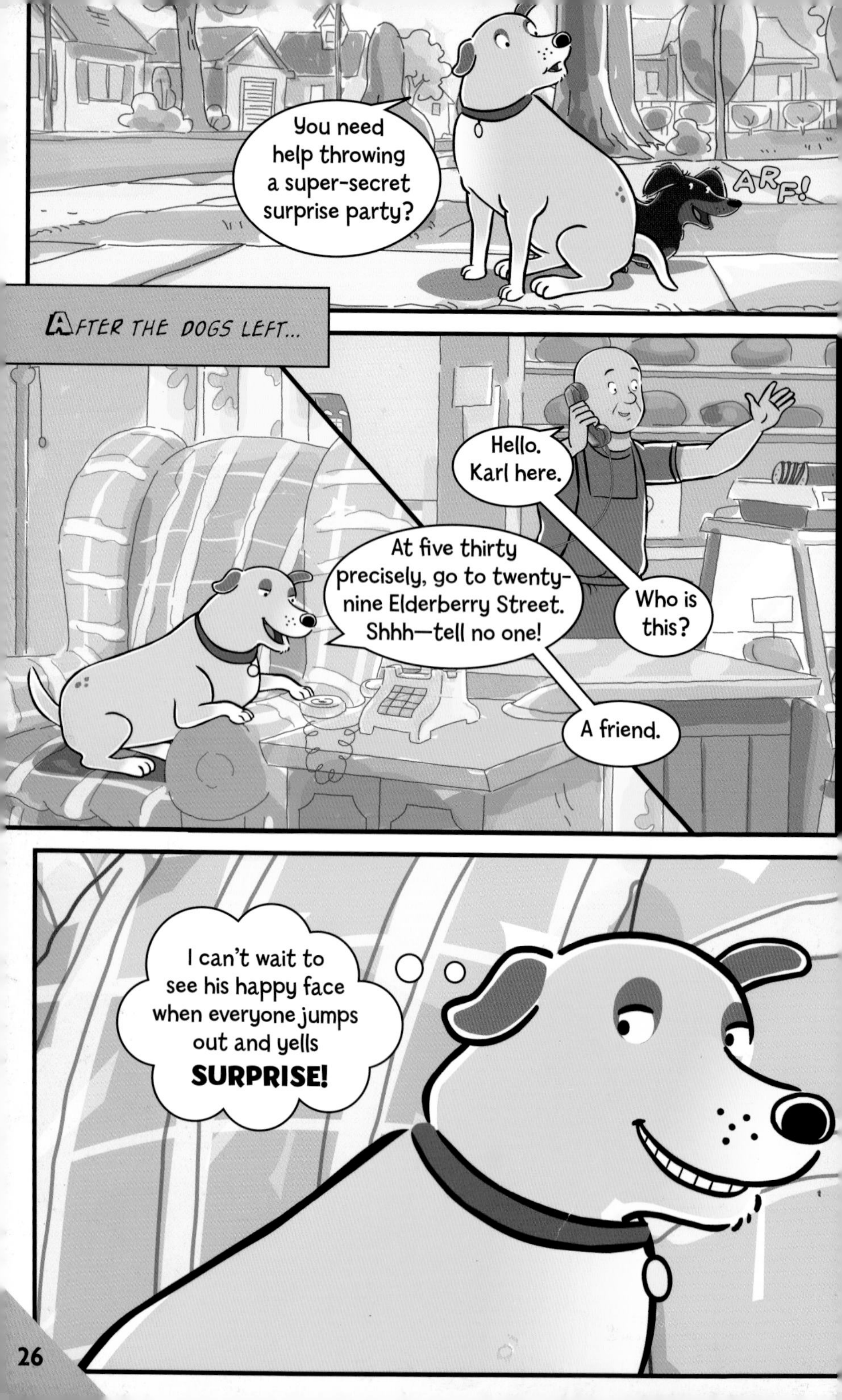
You need help throwing a super-secret surprise party?
ARF!
AFTER THE DOGS LEFT...
Hello. Karl here.
Who is this?
At five thirty precisely, go to twenty-nine Elderberry Street. Shhh—tell no one!
A friend.
I can't wait to see his happy face when everyone jumps out and yells
SURPRISE!

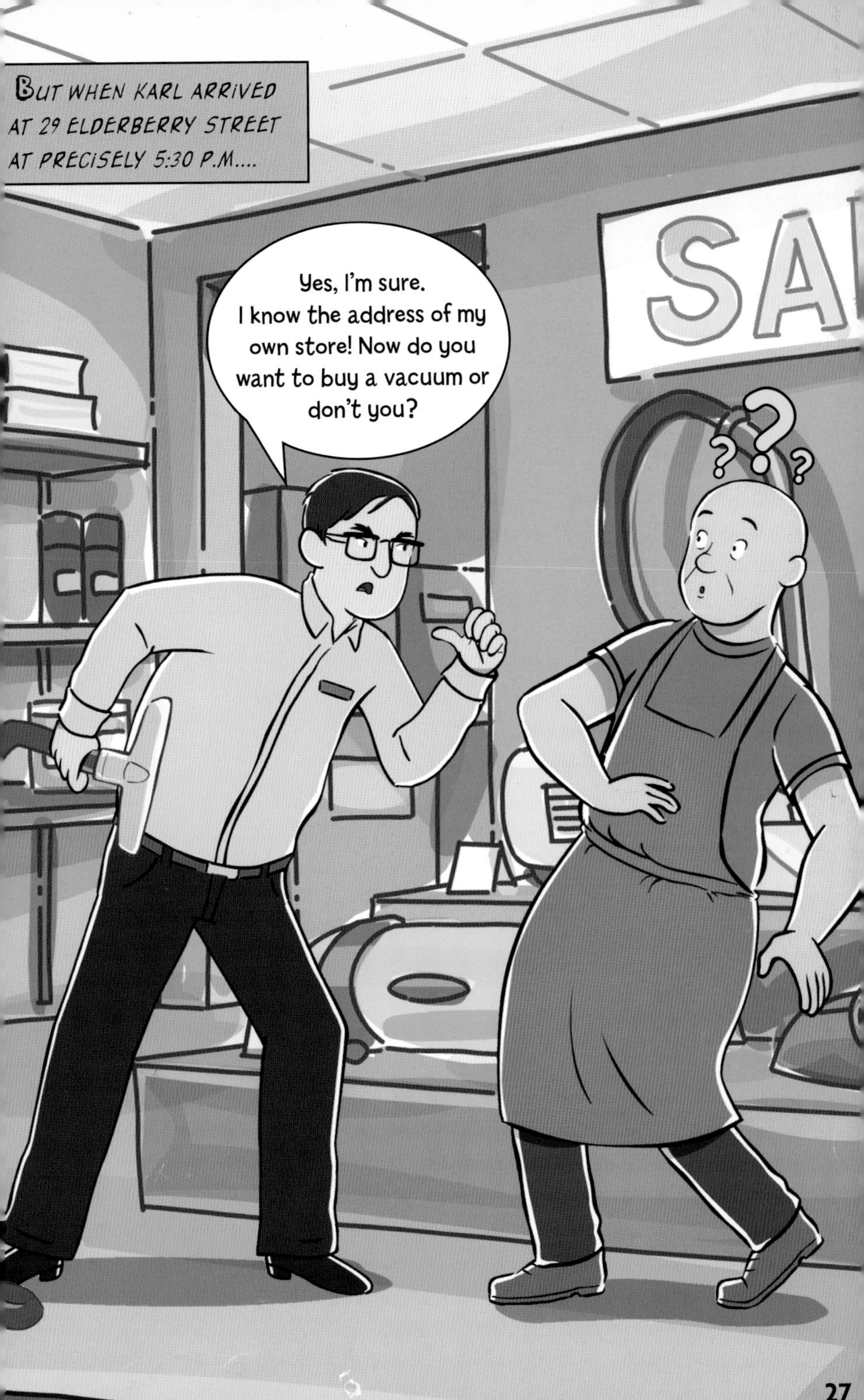

BUT WHEN KARL ARRIVED AT 29 ELDERBERRY STREET AT PRECISELY 5:30 P.M....
Yes, I'm sure. I know the address of my own store! Now do you want to buy a vacuum or don't you?
?

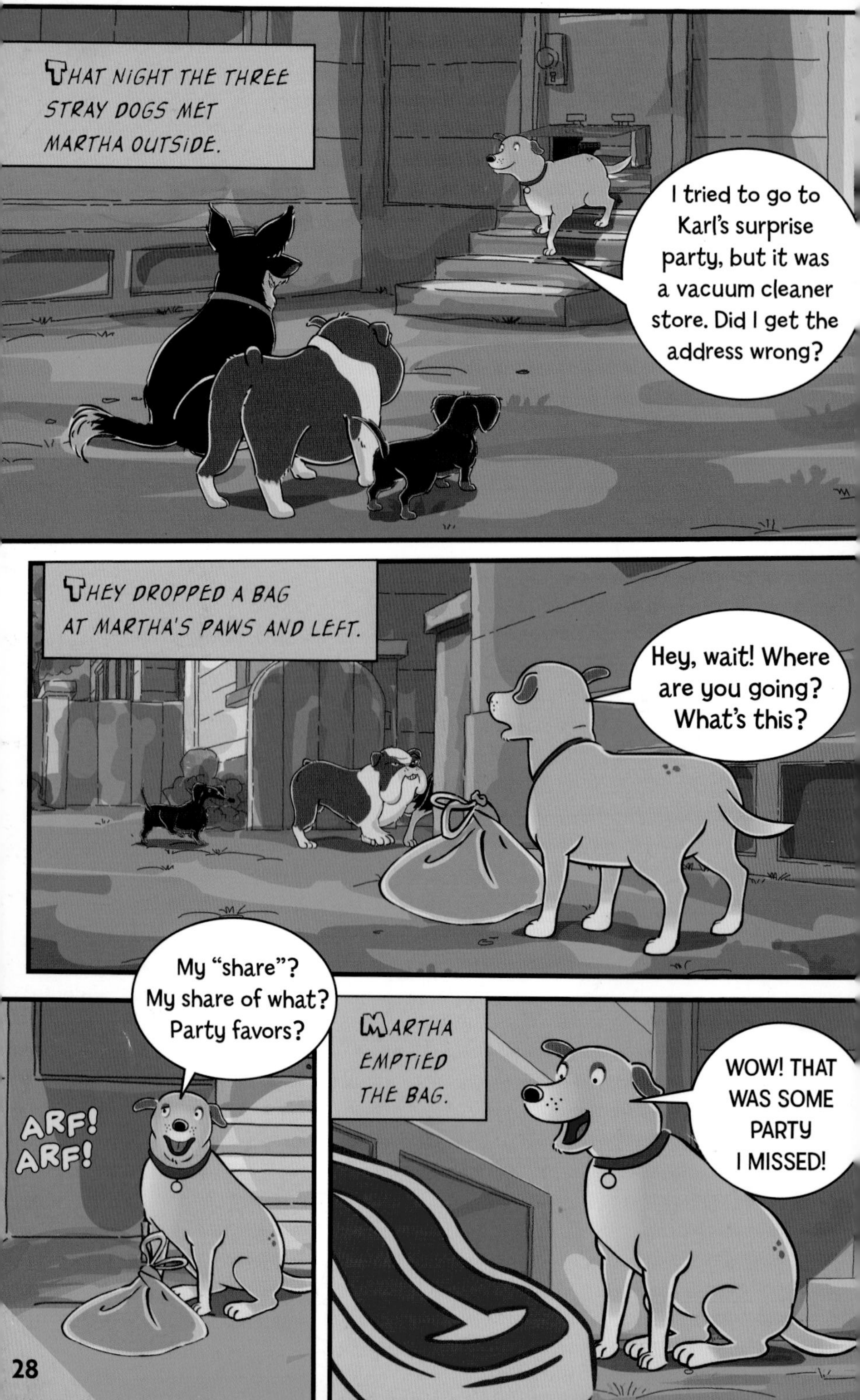
THAT NIGHT THE THREE STRAY DOGS MET MARTHA OUTSIDE.
I tried to go to Karl's surprise party, but it was a vacuum cleaner store. Did I get the address wrong?
THEY DROPPED A BAG AT MARTHA'S PAWS AND LEFT.
Hey, wait! Where are you going? What's this?
ARF! ARF!
My "share"? My share of what? Party favors?
MARTHA EMPTIED THE BAG.
WOW! THAT WAS SOME PARTY I MISSED!

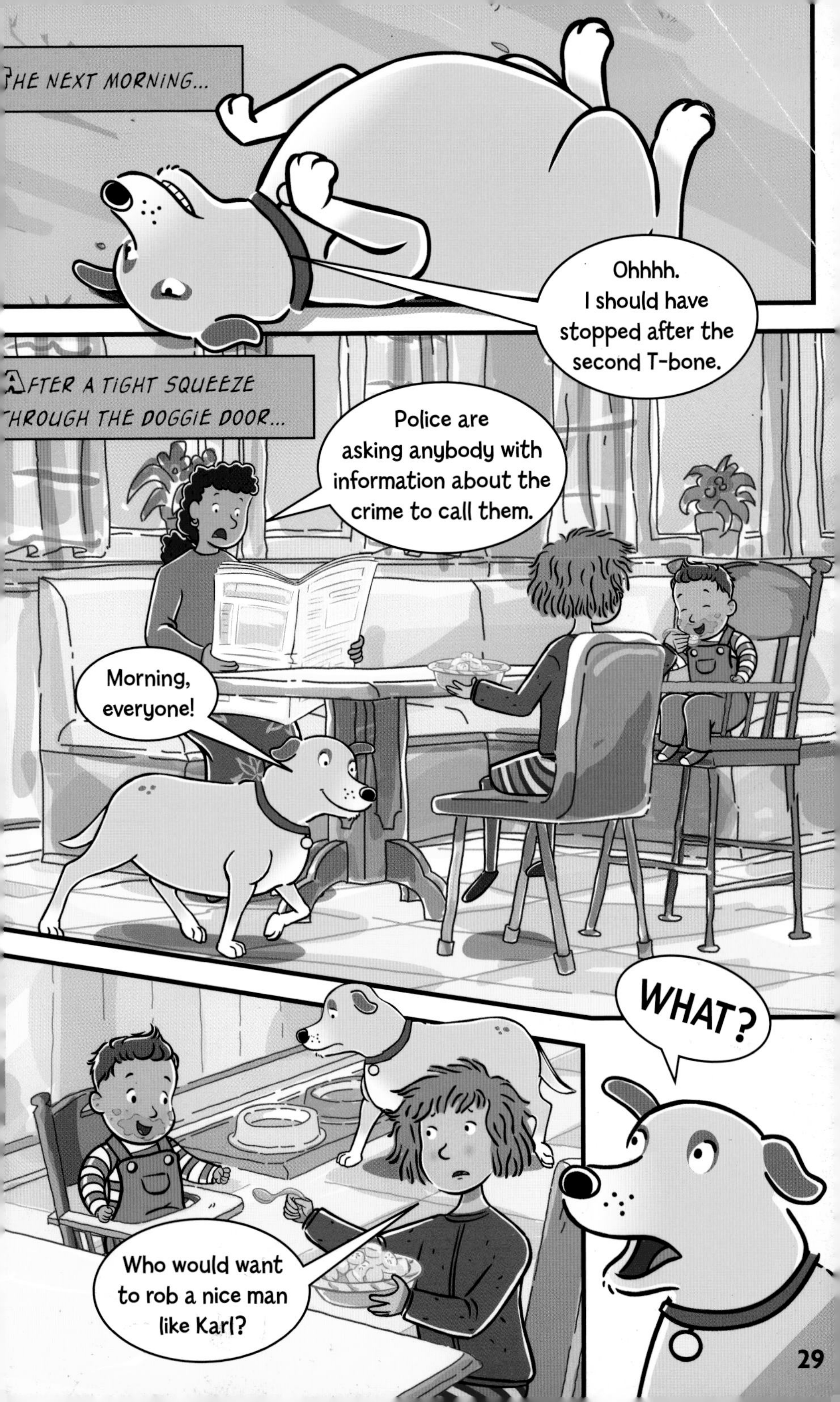
THE NEXT MORNING...
Ohhhh. I should have stopped after the second T-bone.
AFTER A TIGHT SQUEEZE THROUGH THE DOGGIE DOOR...
Police are asking anybody with information about the crime to call them.
Morning, everyone!
WHAT?
Who would want to rob a nice man like Karl?

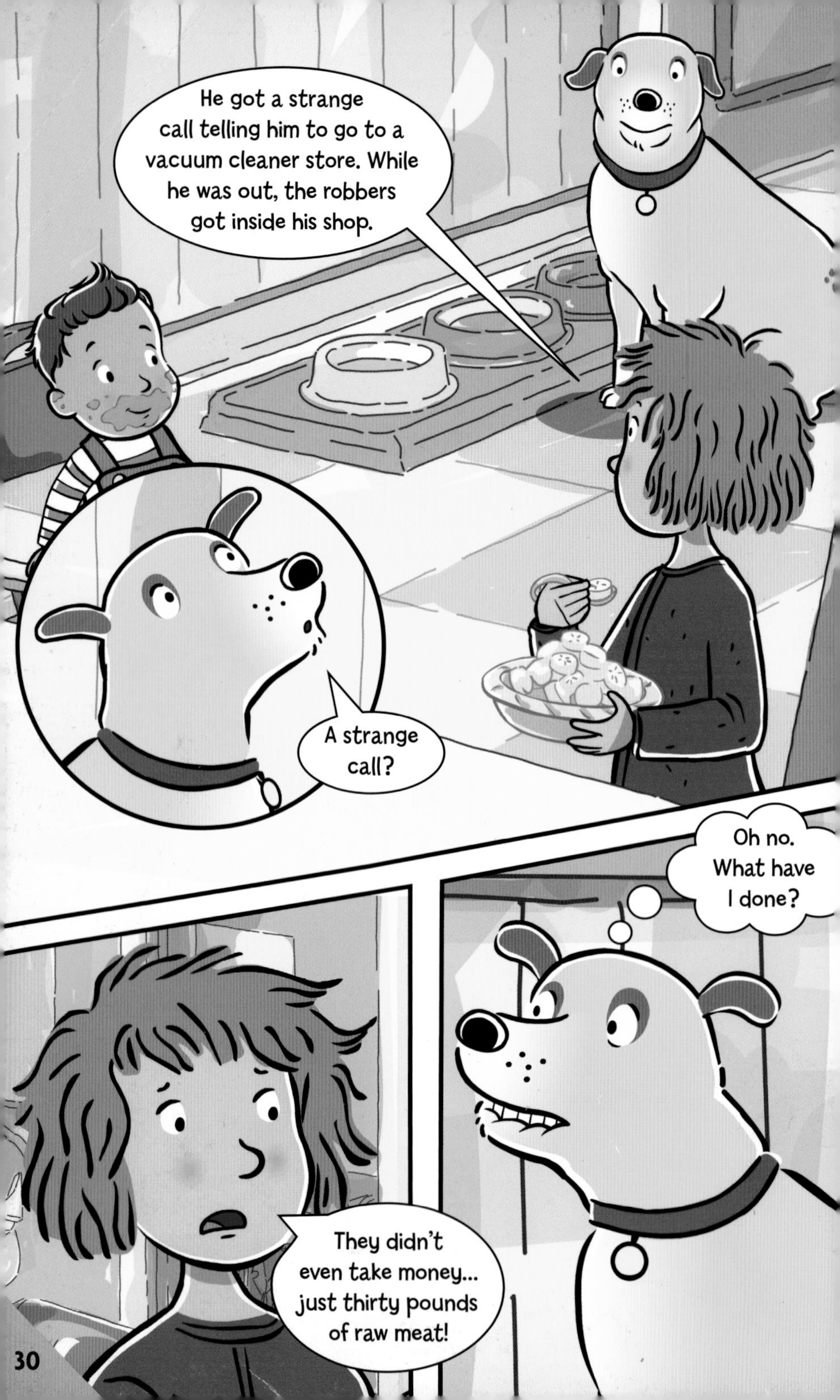
He got a strange call telling him to go to a vacuum cleaner store. While he was out, the robbers got inside his shop.
A strange call?
Oh no. What have I done?
They didn't even take money... just thirty pounds of raw meat!

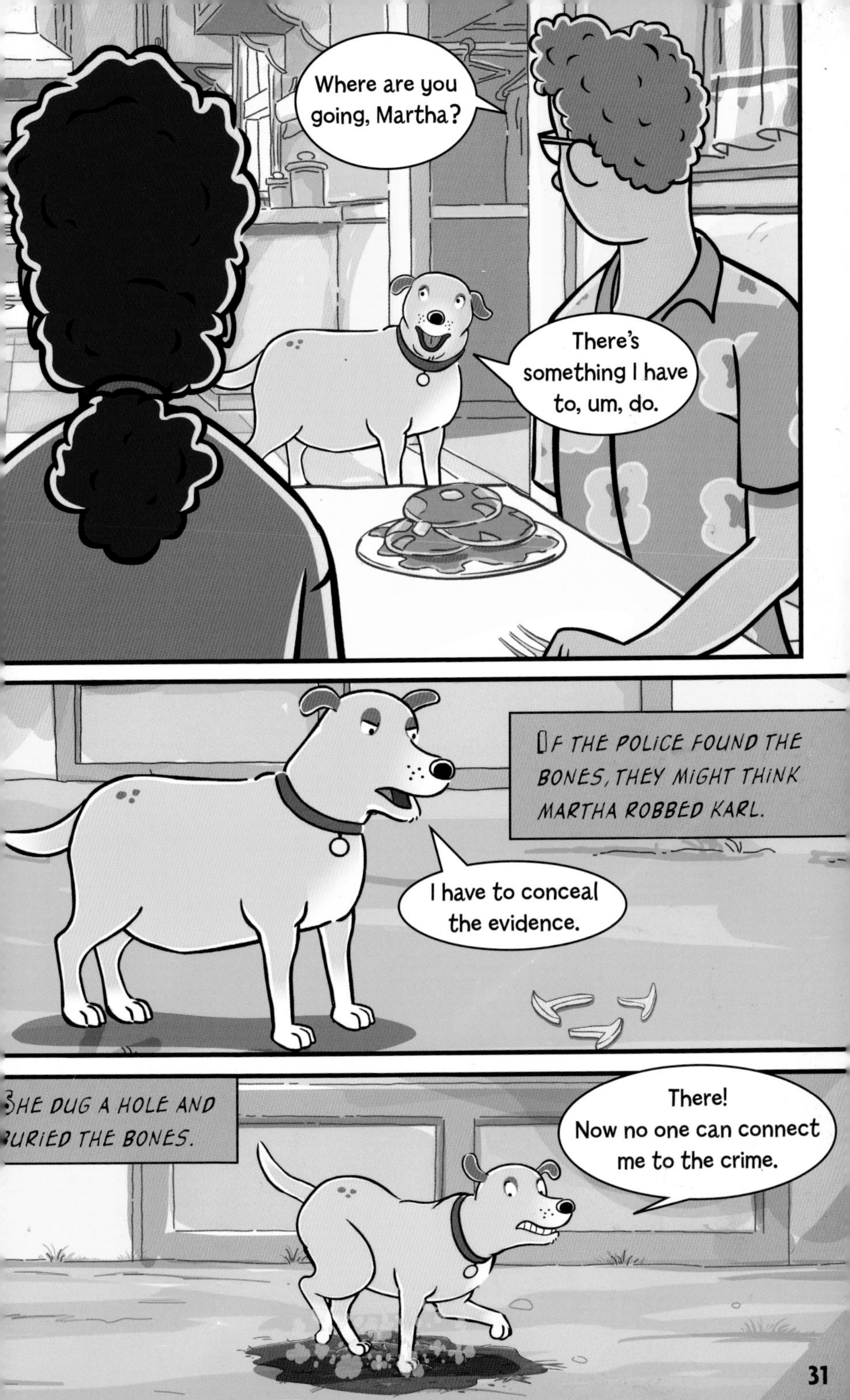
Where are you going, Martha?
There's something I have to, um, do.
IF THE POLICE FOUND THE BONES, THEY MIGHT THINK MARTHA ROBBED KARL.
I have to conceal the evidence.
SHE DUG A HOLE AND BURIED THE BONES.
There! Now no one can connect me to the crime.

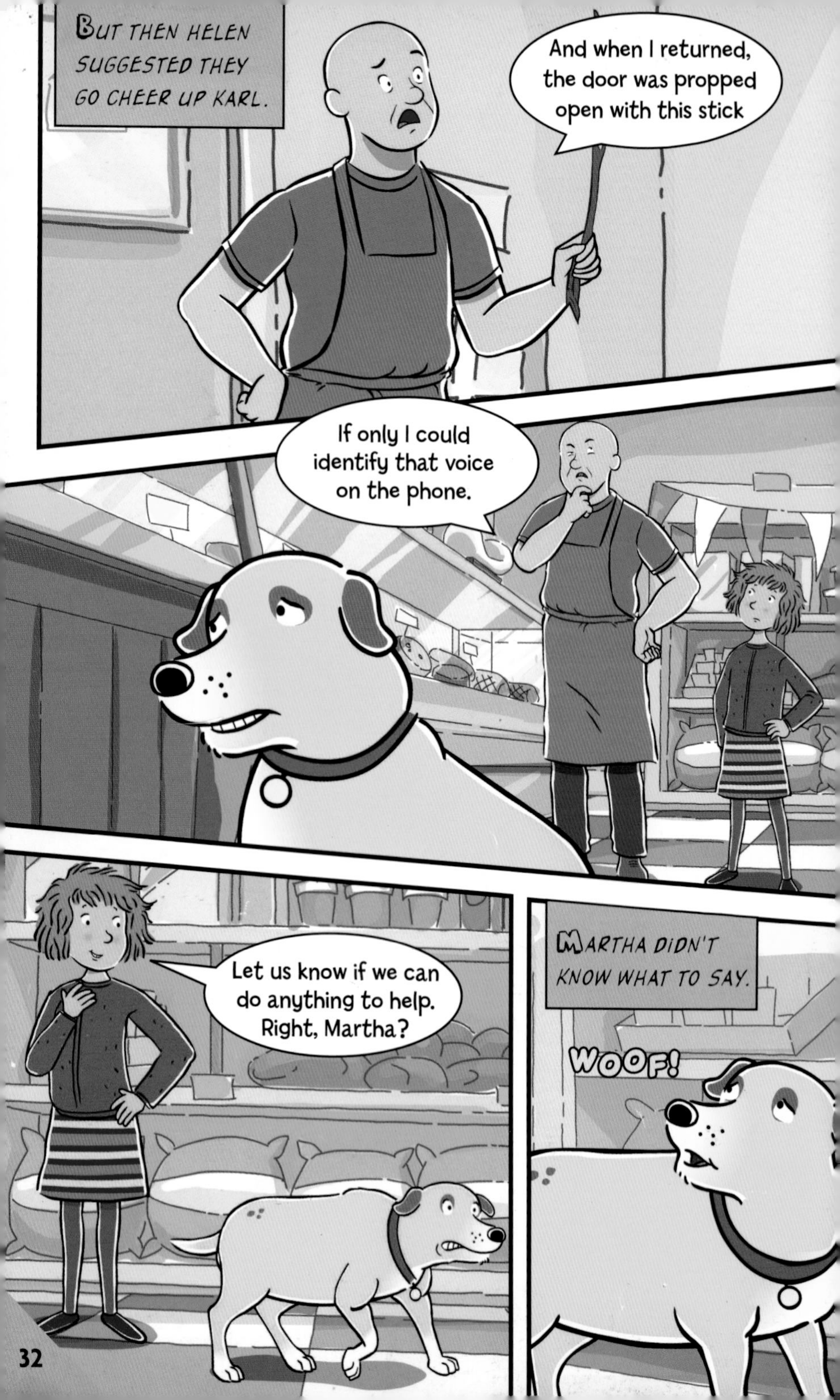
BUT THEN HELEN SUGGESTED THEY GO CHEER UP KARL.
And when I returned, the door was propped open with this stick
If only I could identify that voice on the phone.
Let us know if we can do anything to help. Right, Martha?
MARTHA DIDN'T KNOW WHAT TO SAY.
WOOF!

33

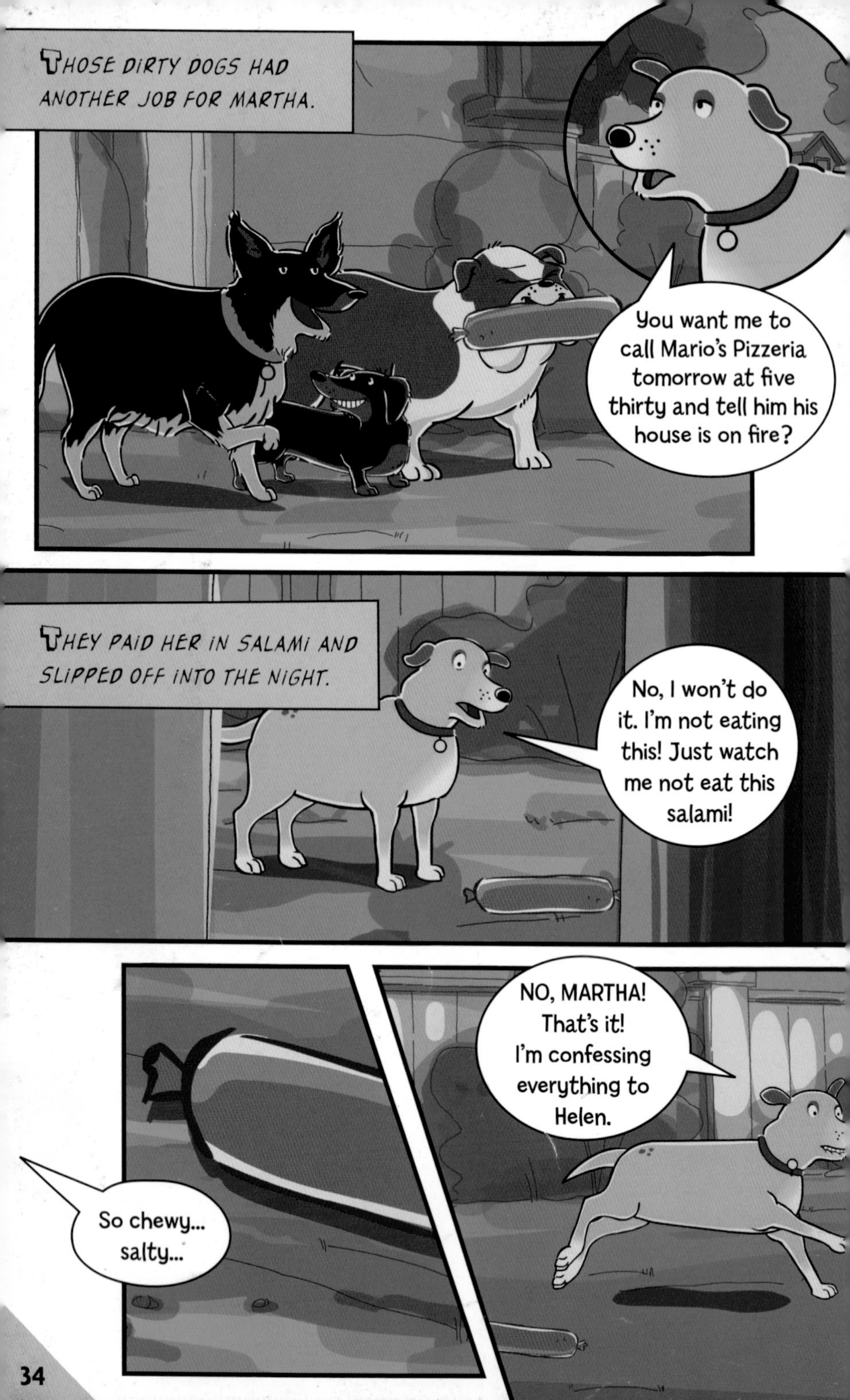
THOSE DIRTY DOGS HAD ANOTHER JOB FOR MARTHA.
You want me to call Mario's Pizzeria tomorrow at five thirty and tell him his house is on fire?
THEY PAID HER IN SALAMI AND SLIPPED OFF INTO THE NIGHT.
No, I won't do it. I'm not eating this! Just watch me not eat this salami!
So chewy... salty...
NO, MARTHA! That's it! I'm confessing everything to Helen.

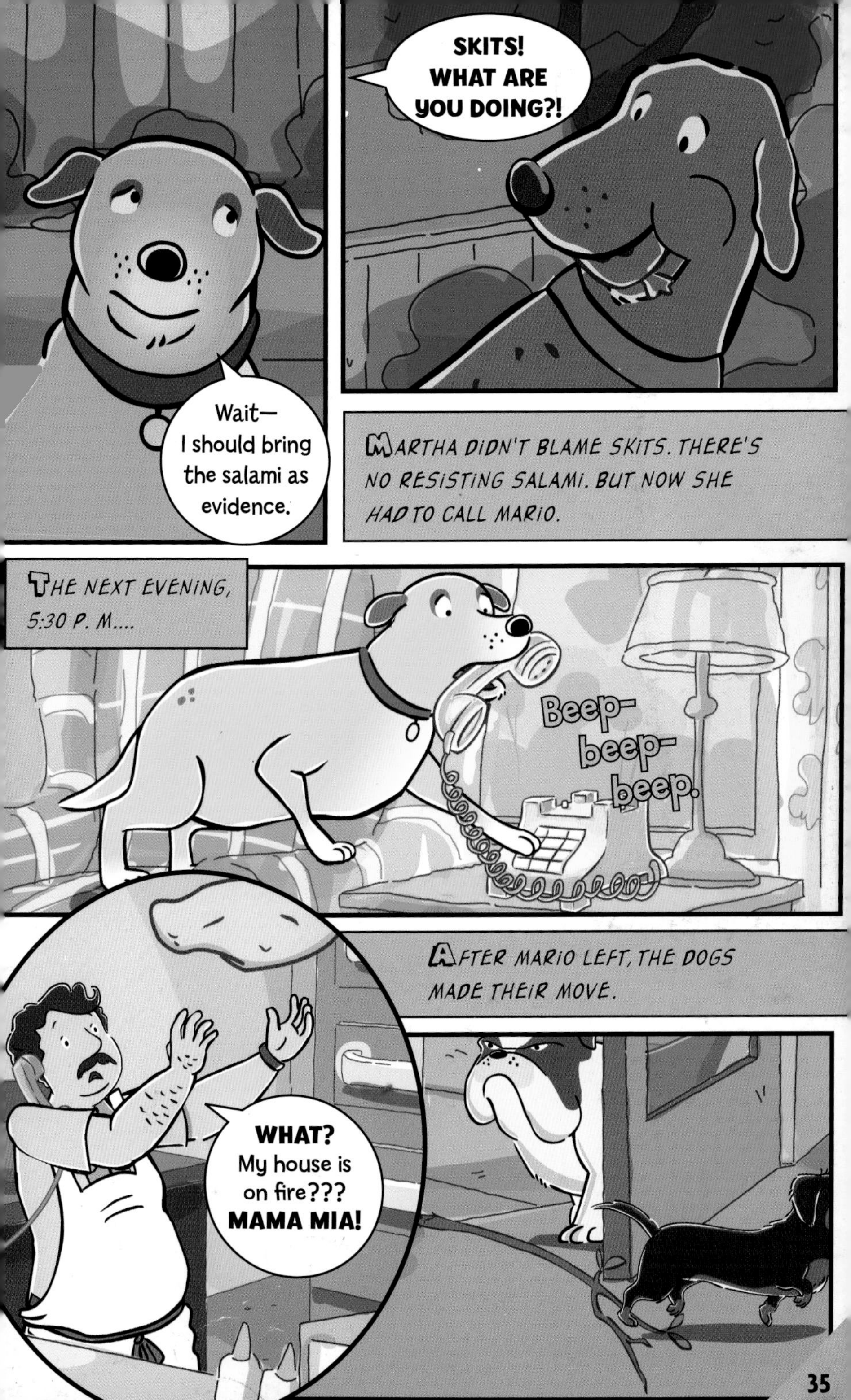

Wait— I should bring the salami as evidence.
SKITS! WHAT ARE YOU DOING?!
MARTHA DIDN'T BLAME SKITS. THERE'S NO RESISTING SALAMI. BUT NOW SHE HAD TO CALL MARIO.
THE NEXT EVENING, 5:30 P. M....
Beep-beep-beep.
WHAT? My house is on fire??? MAMA MIA!
AFTER MARIO LEFT, THE DOGS MADE THEIR MOVE.

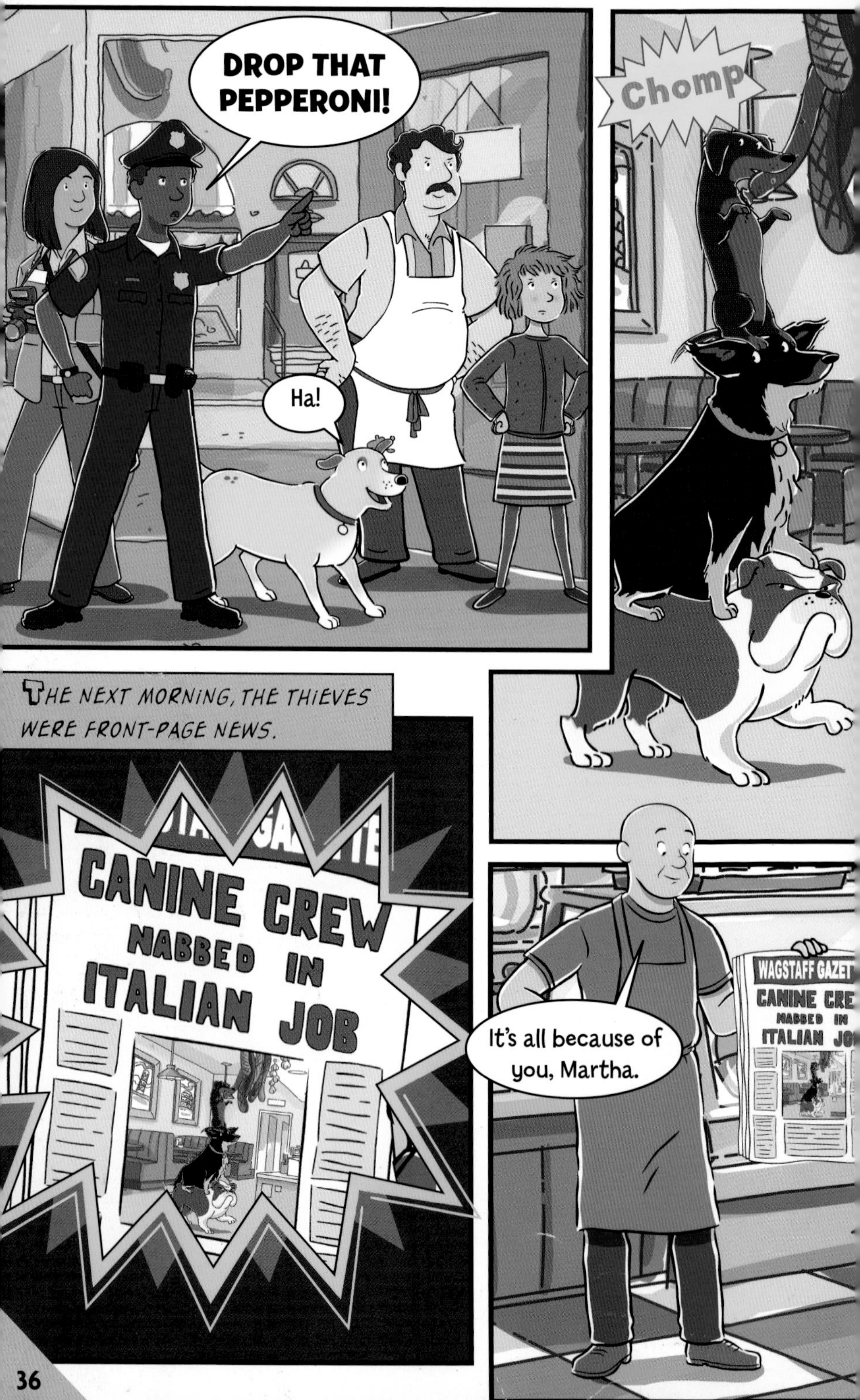
DROP THAT PEPPERONI!
Ha!
Chomp
THE NEXT MORNING, THE THIEVES WERE FRONT-PAGE NEWS.
CANINE CREW NABBED IN ITALIAN JOB
It's all because of you, Martha.

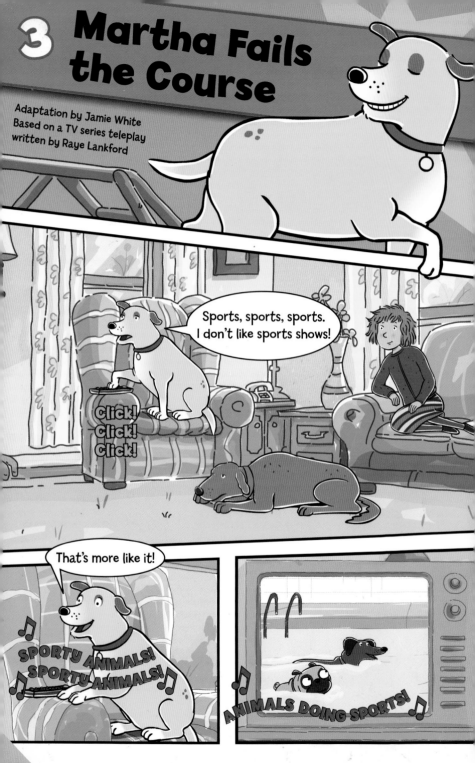

3 Martha Fails the Course

Adaptation by Jamie White
Based on a TV series teleplay
written by Raye Lankford

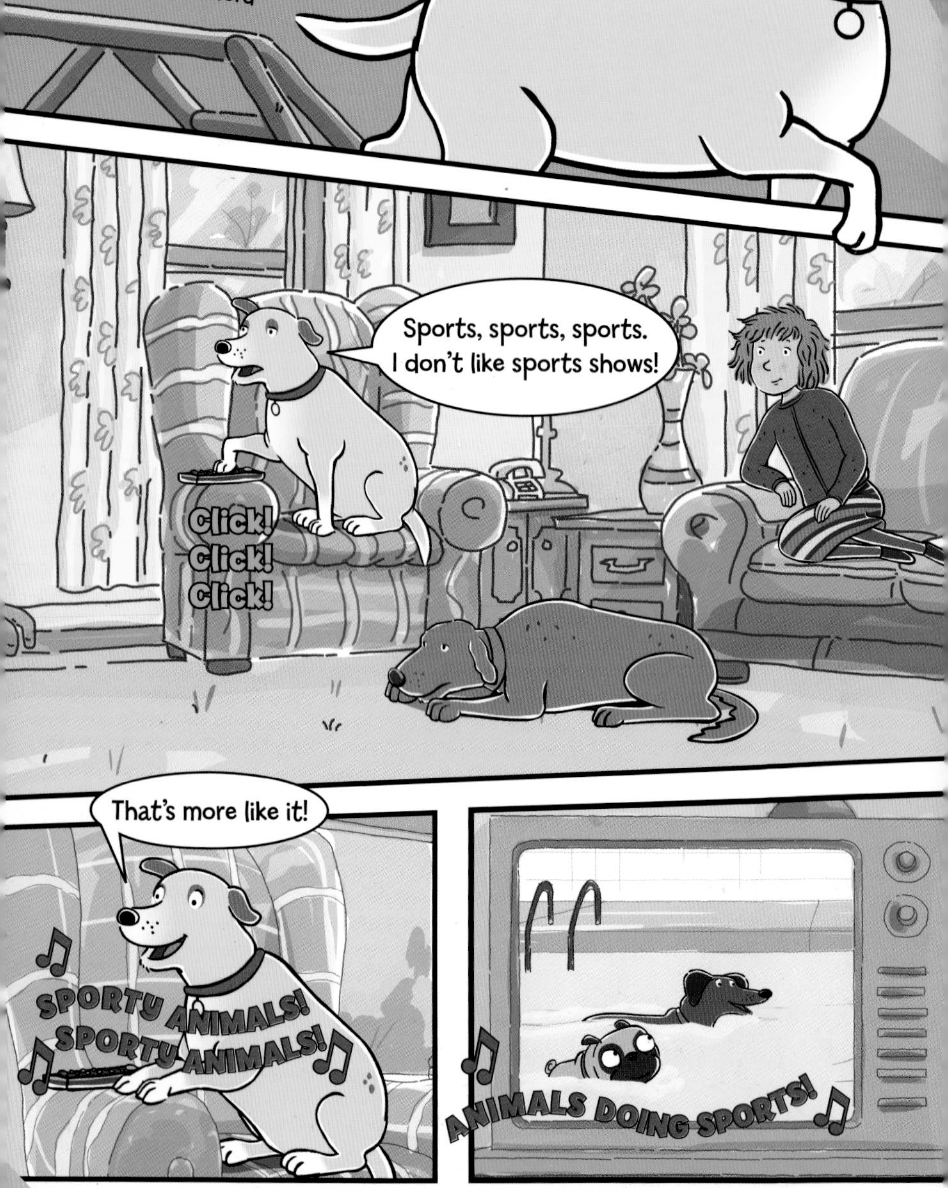

Sports, sports, sports. I don't like sports shows!
Click! Click! Click!
That's more like it!
SPORTY ANIMALS! SPORTY ANIMALS!
ANIMALS DOING SPORTS!

39

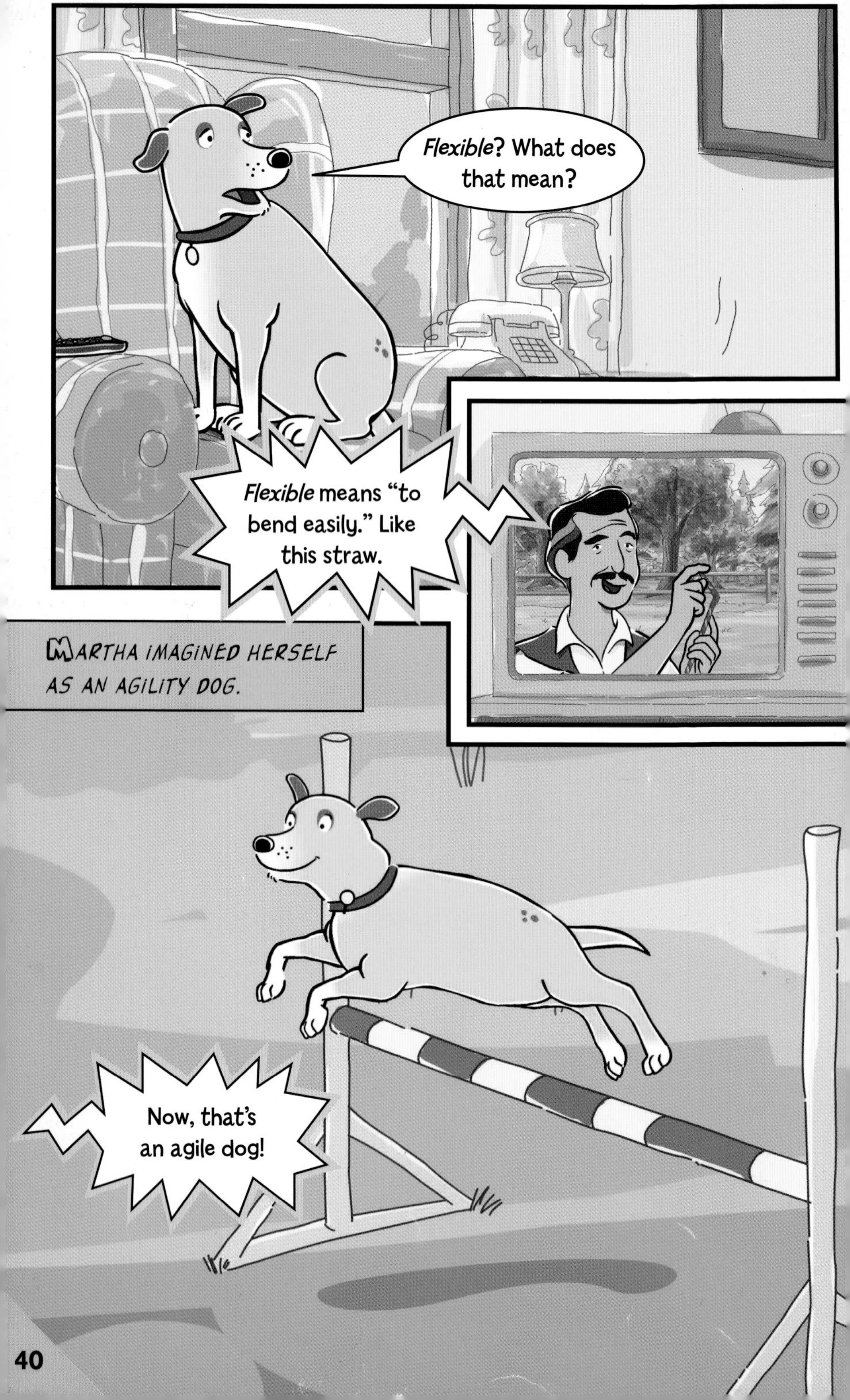

Flexible? What does that mean?
Flexible means "to bend easily." Like this straw.
MARTHA IMAGINED HERSELF AS AN AGILITY DOG.
Now, that's an agile dog!

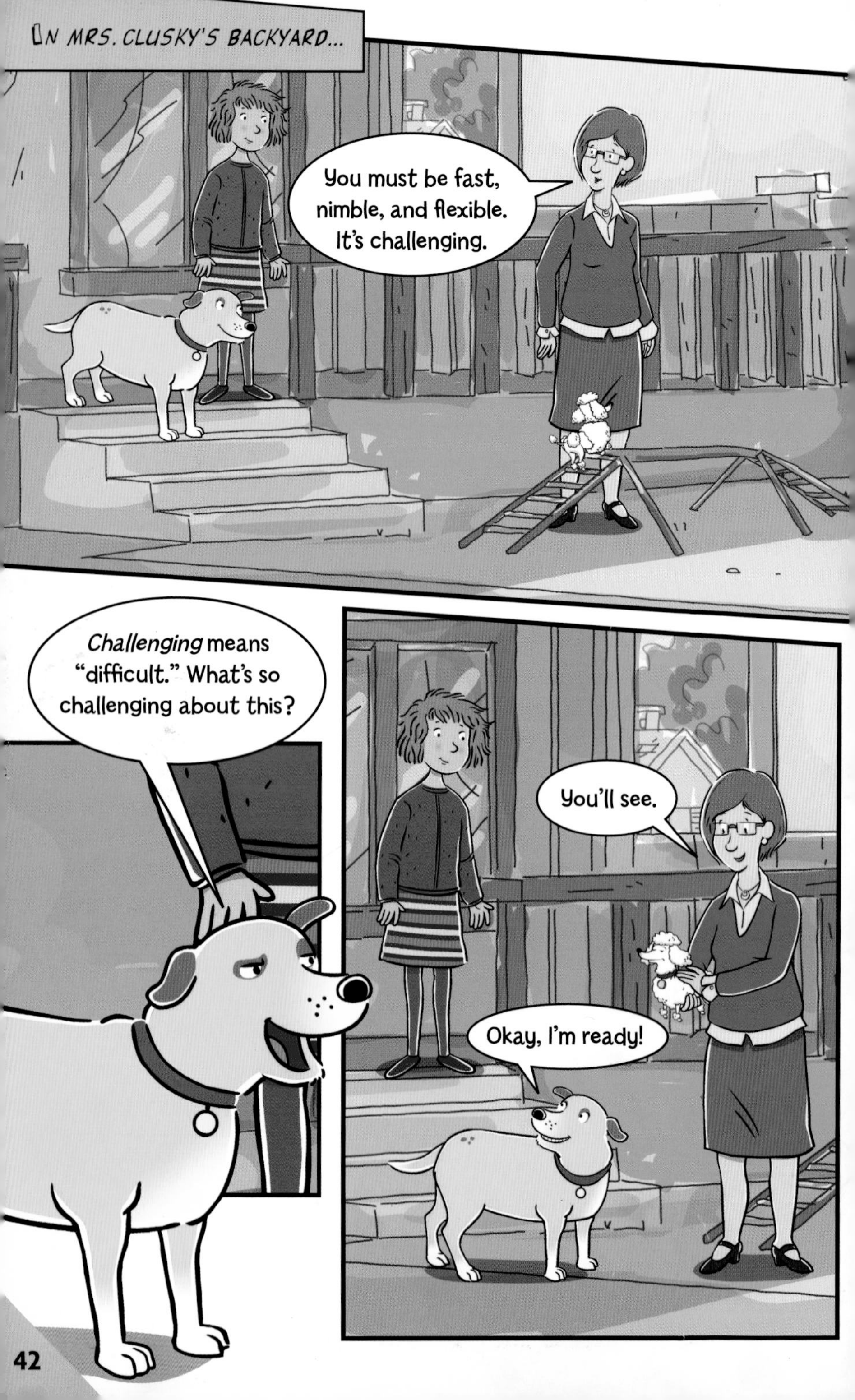
IN MRS. CLUSKY'S BACKYARD...
You must be fast, nimble, and flexible. It's challenging.
Challenging means "difficult." What's so challenging about this?
You'll see.
Okay, I'm ready!

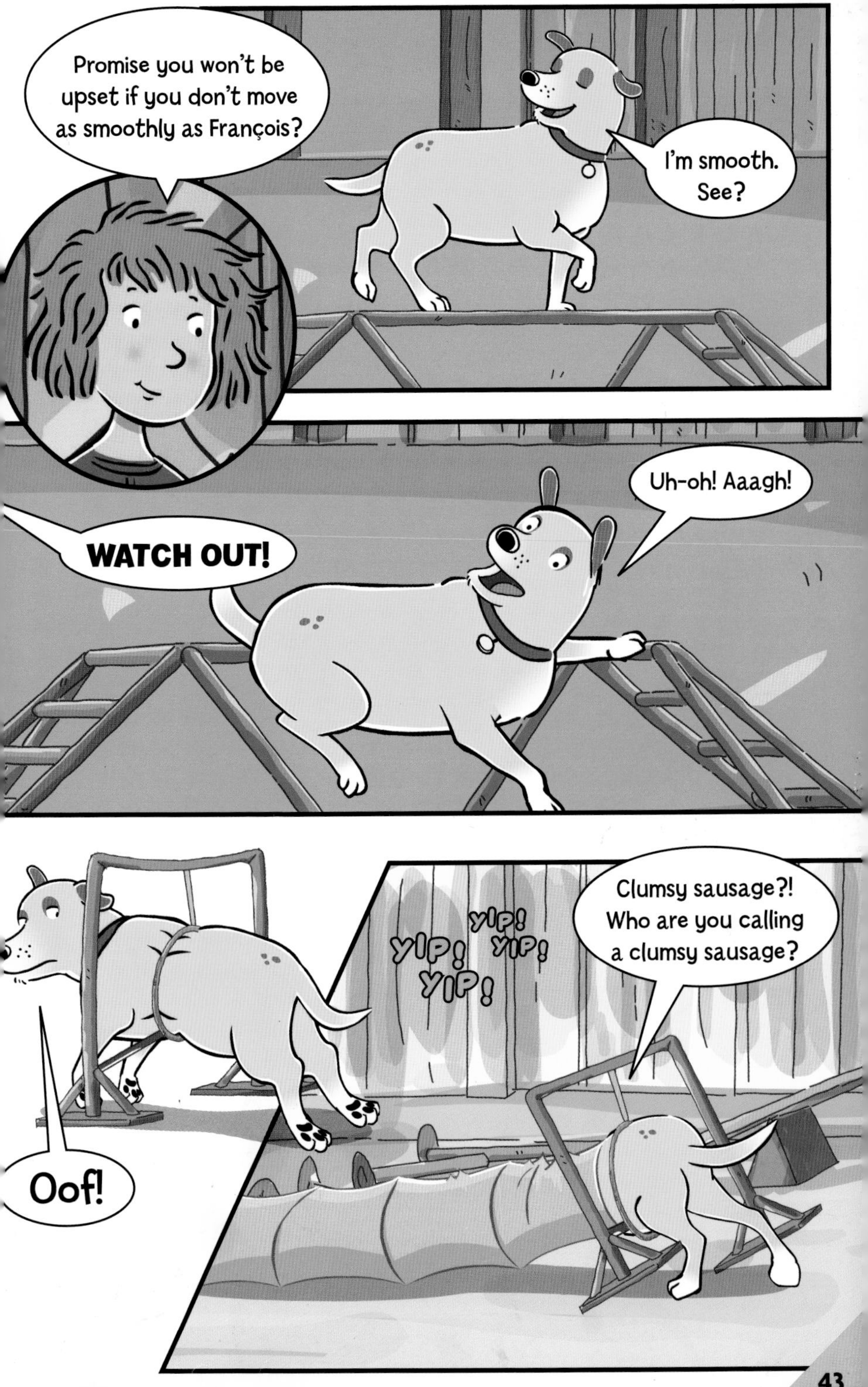

Promise you won't be upset if you don't move as smoothly as François?
I'm smooth. See?
Uh-oh! Aaagh!
WATCH OUT!
YIP! YIP! YIP! YIP!
Clumsy sausage?! Who are you calling a clumsy sausage?
Oof!

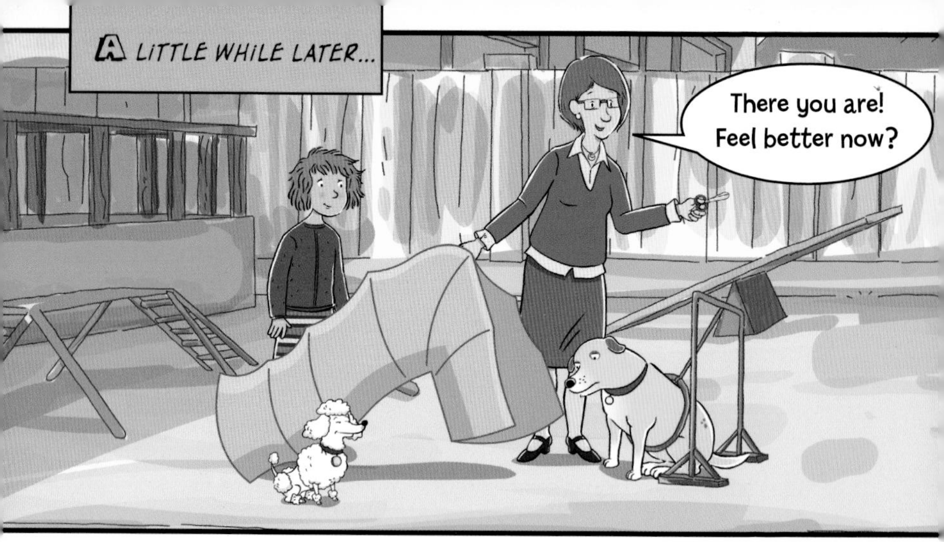
A LITTLE WHILE LATER...
There you are!
Feel better now?

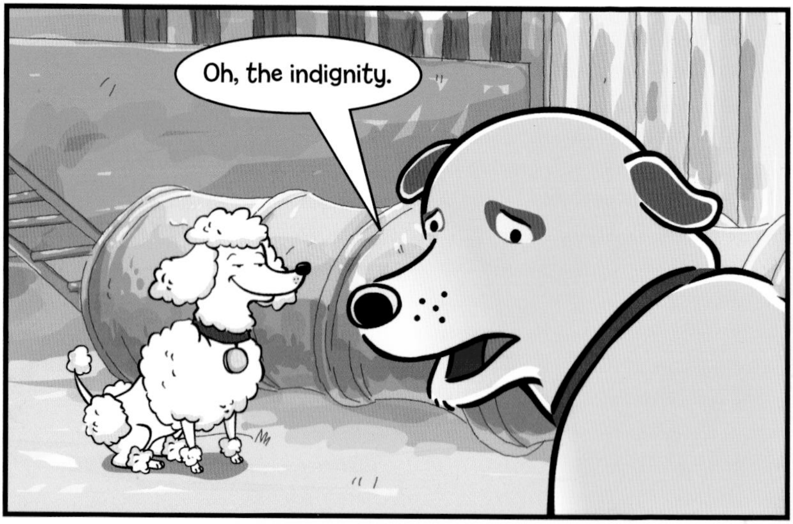
Oh, the indignity.

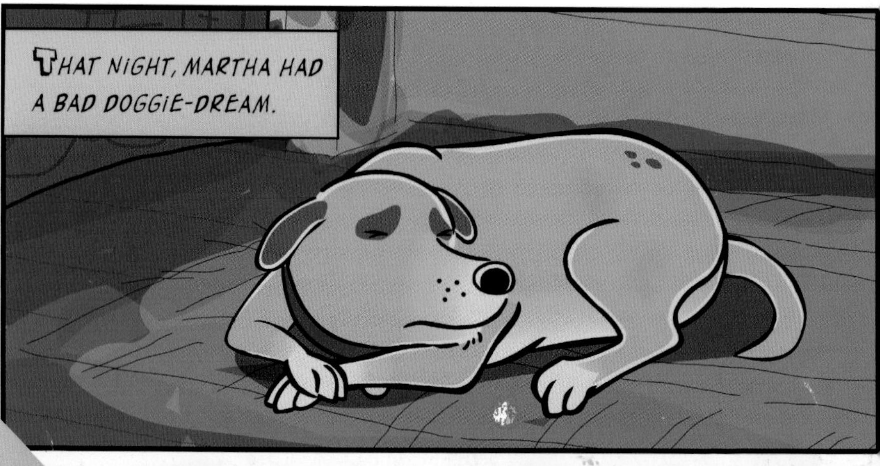
THAT NIGHT, MARTHA HAD
A BAD DOGGIE-DREAM.

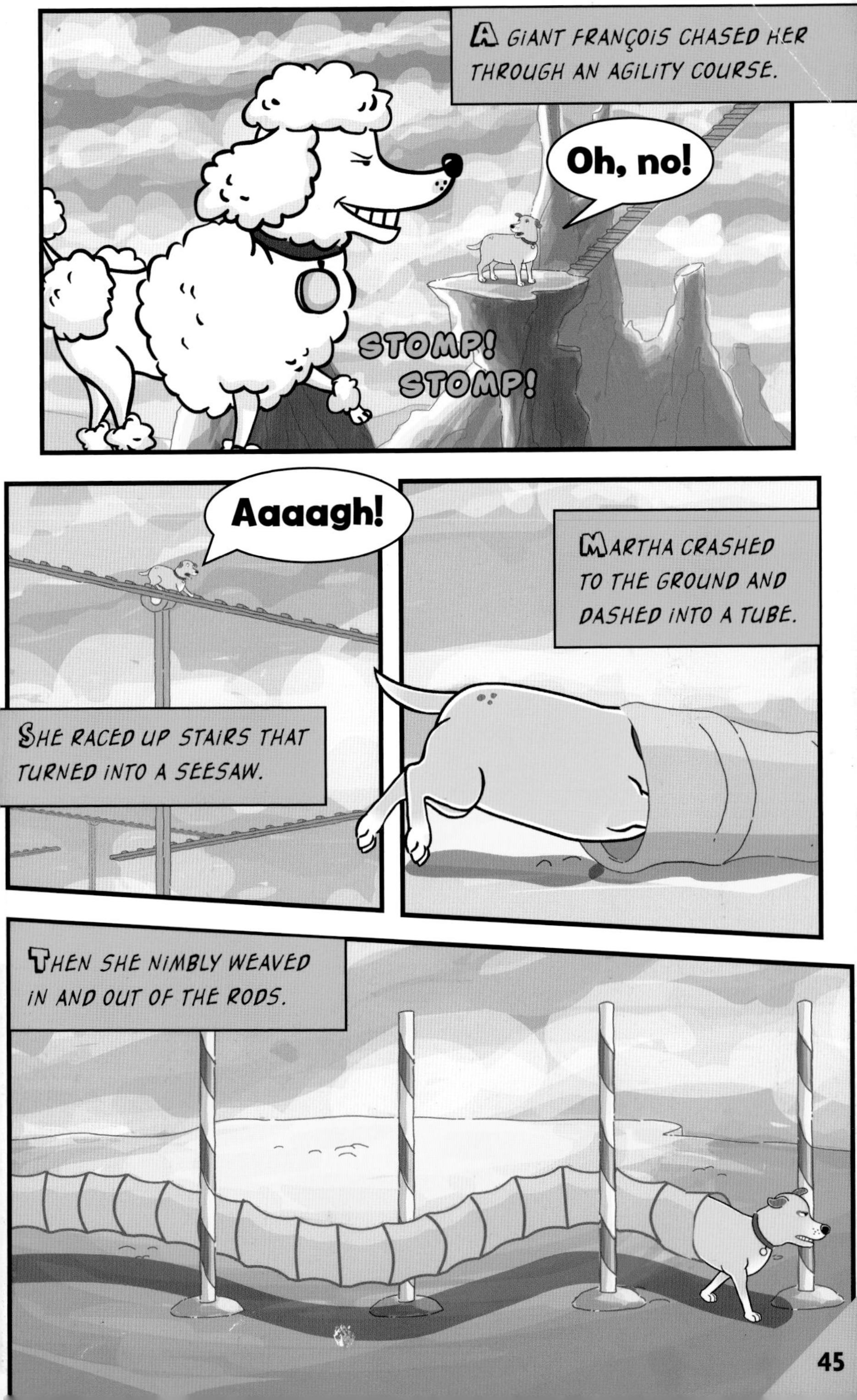

A GIANT FRANÇOIS CHASED HER THROUGH AN AGILITY COURSE.
Oh, no!
STOMP! STOMP!
Aaaagh!
SHE RACED UP STAIRS THAT TURNED INTO A SEESAW.
MARTHA CRASHED TO THE GROUND AND DASHED INTO A TUBE.
THEN SHE NIMBLY WEAVED IN AND OUT OF THE RODS.

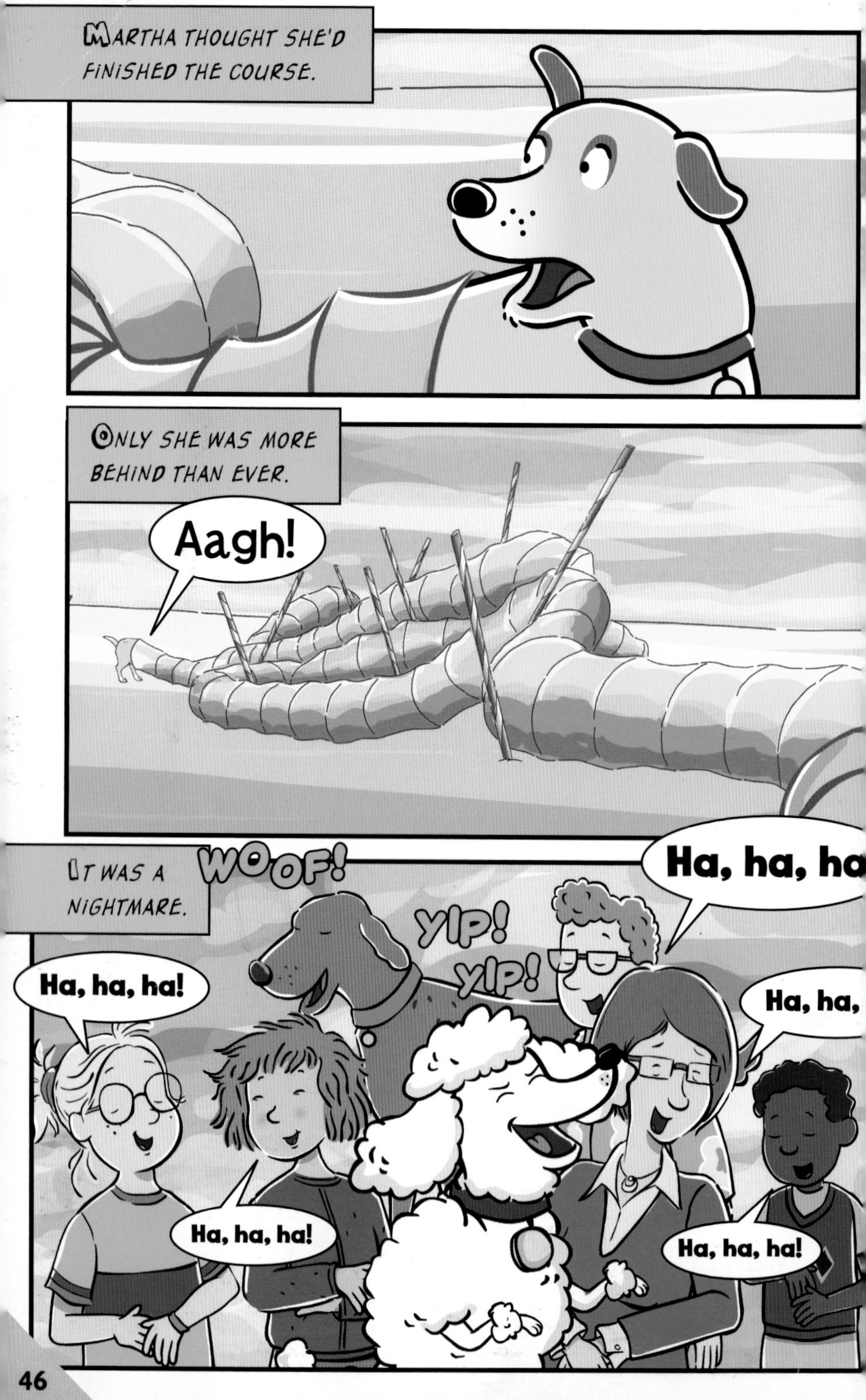

MARTHA THOUGHT SHE'D FINISHED THE COURSE.
ONLY SHE WAS MORE BEHIND THAN EVER.
Aagh!
IT WAS A NIGHTMARE.
WOOF!
Ha, ha, ha
YIP! YIP!
Ha, ha, ha!
Ha, ha,
Ha, ha, ha!
Ha, ha, ha!

47

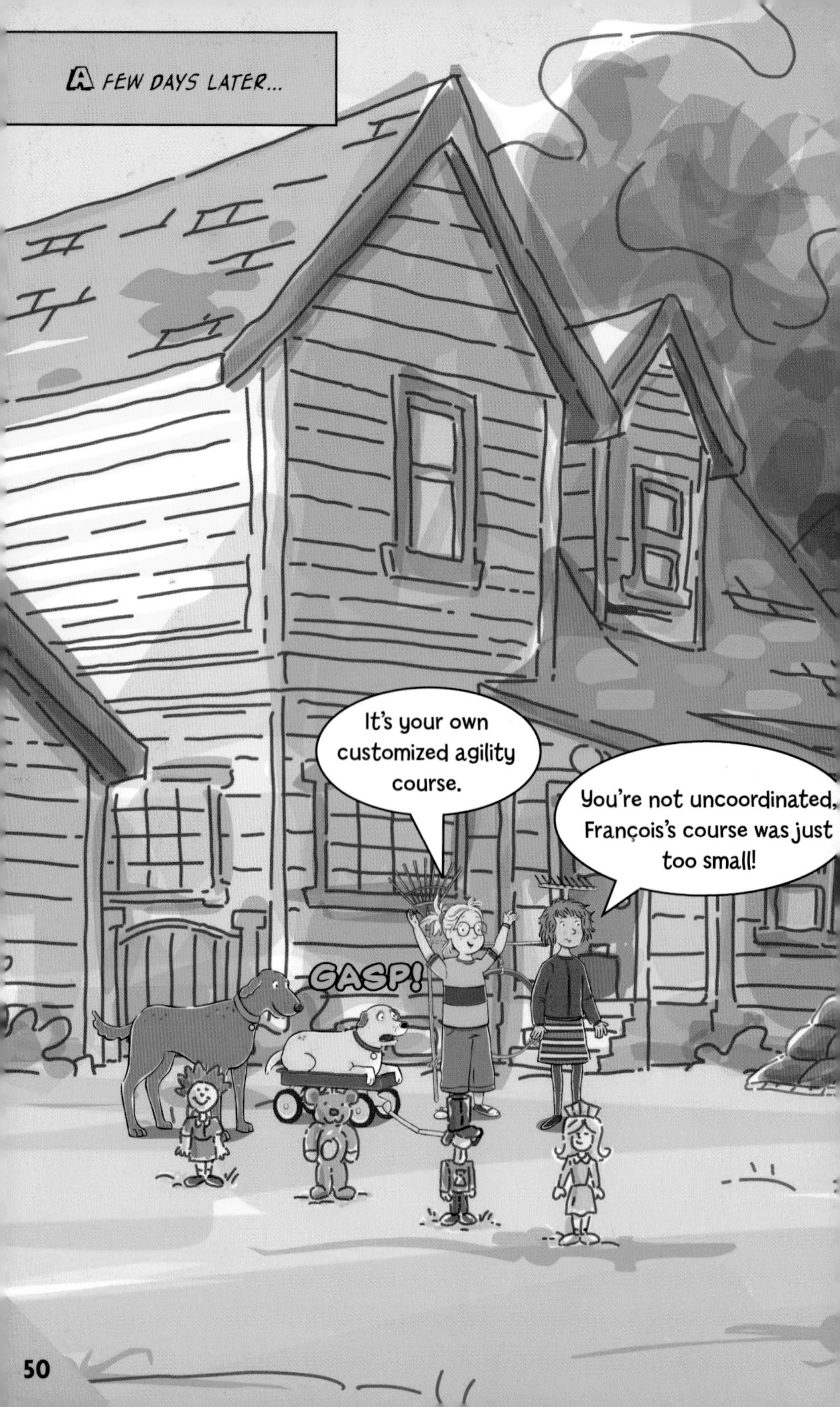
A FEW DAYS LATER...
It's your own customized agility course.
You're not uncoordinated, François's course was just too small!
GASP!

51

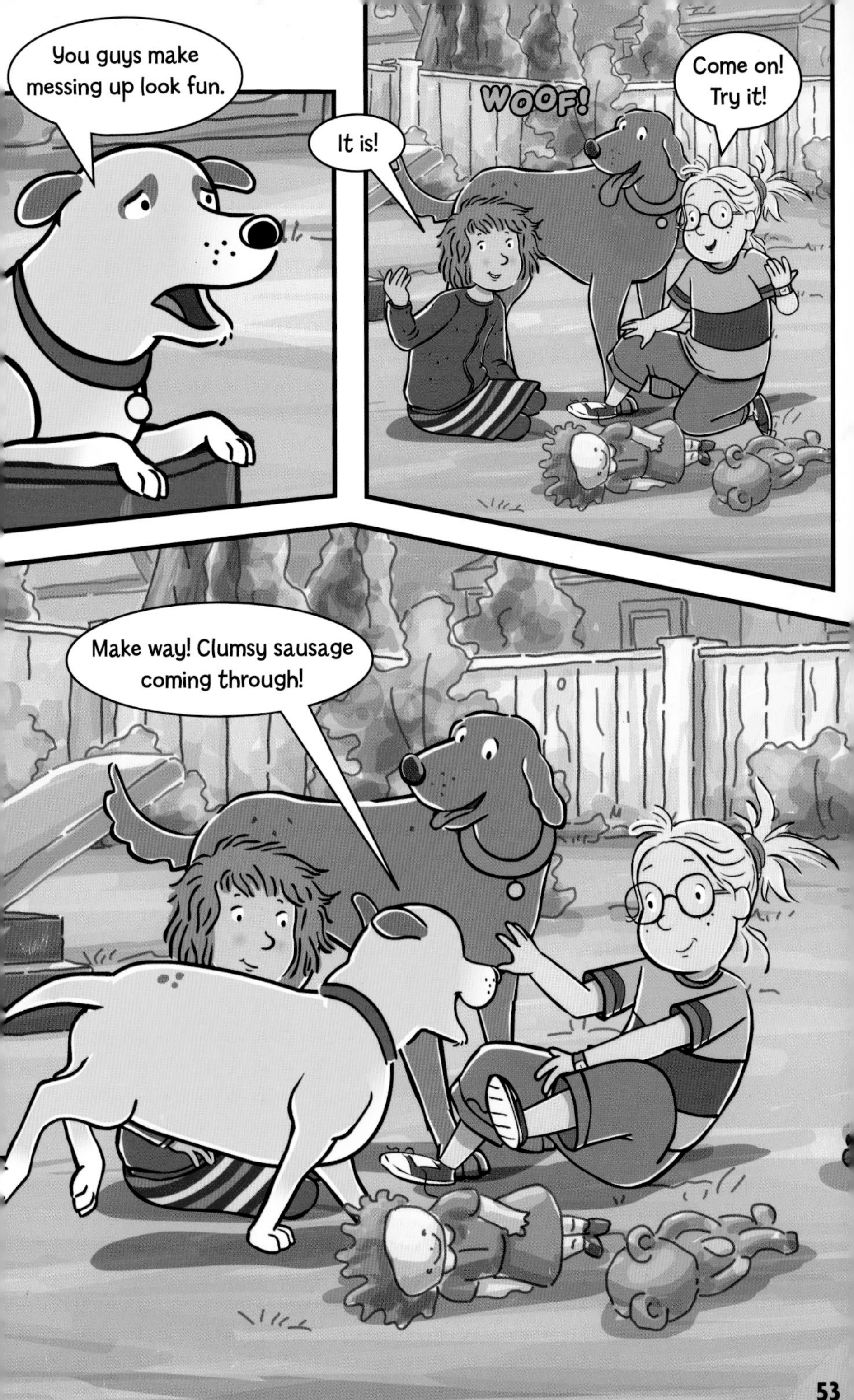
You guys make messing up look fun.
It is!
WOOF!
Come on! Try it!
Make way! Clumsy sausage coming through!

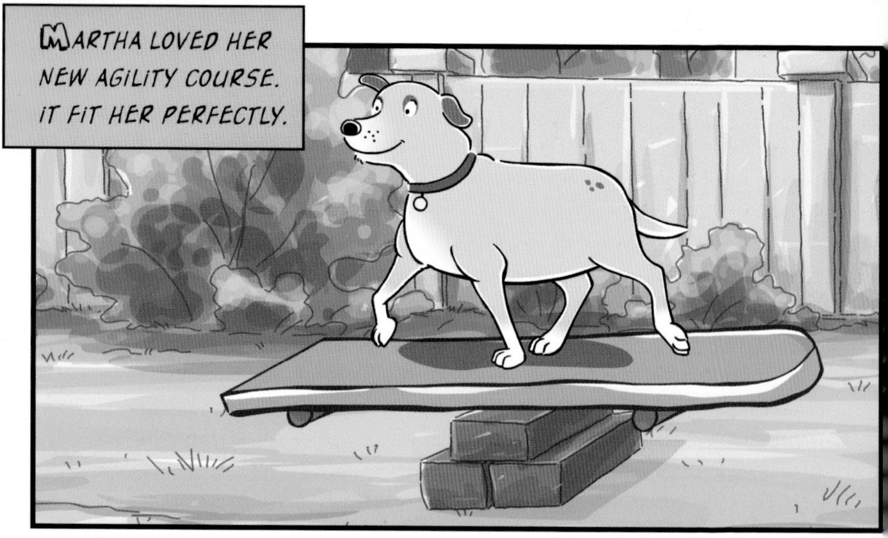
MARTHA LOVED HER NEW AGILITY COURSE. IT FIT HER PERFECTLY.

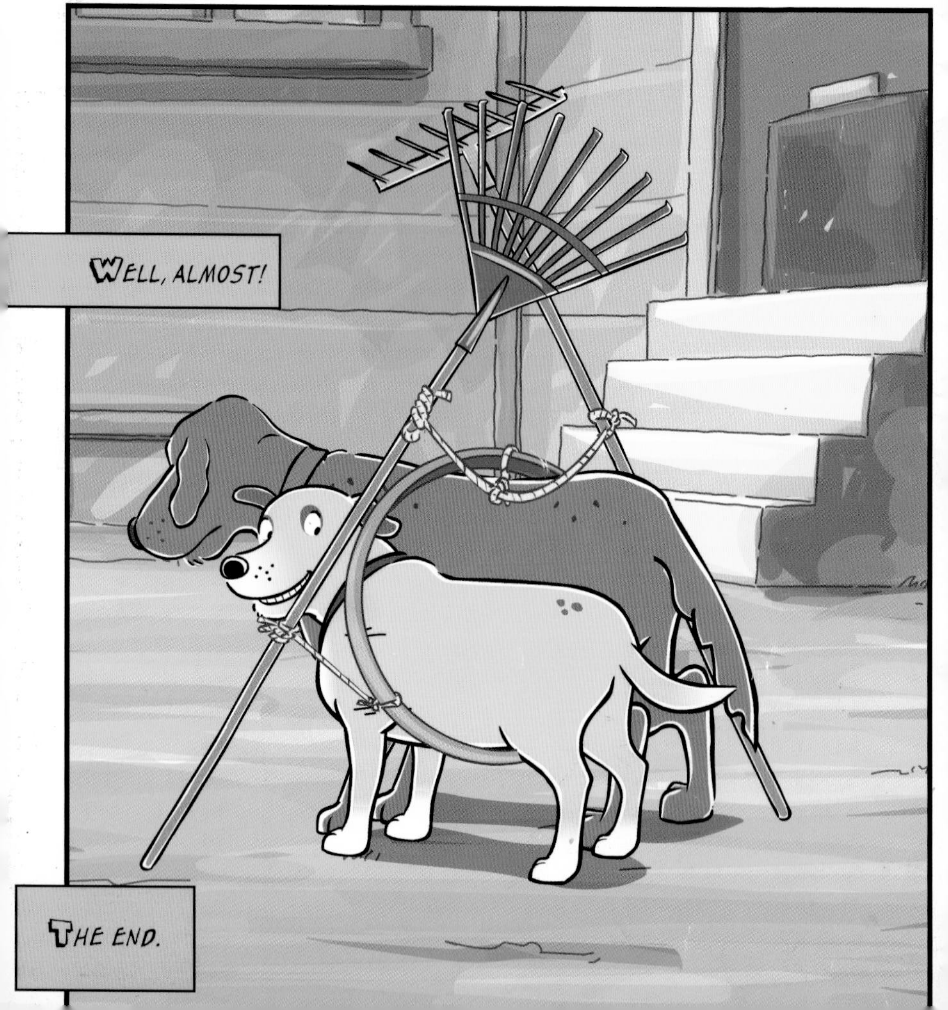
WELL, ALMOST!
THE END.

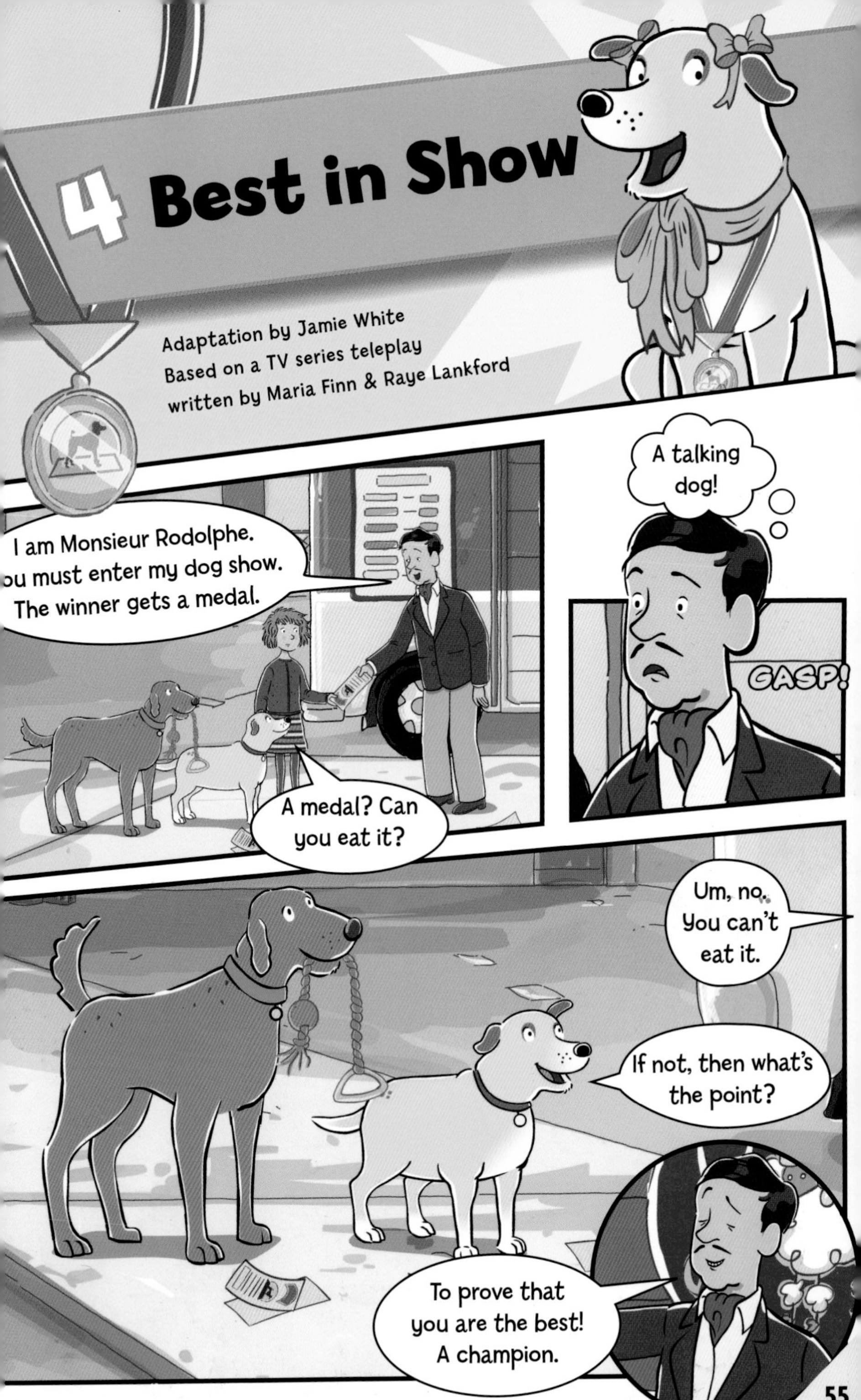
4 Best in Show
Adaptation by Jamie White
Based on a TV series teleplay
written by Maria Finn & Raye Lankford
I am Monsieur Rodolphe. ou must enter my dog show. The winner gets a medal.
A medal? Can you eat it?
A talking dog!
GASP!
Um, no. You can't eat it.
If not, then what's the point?
To prove that you are the best! A champion.

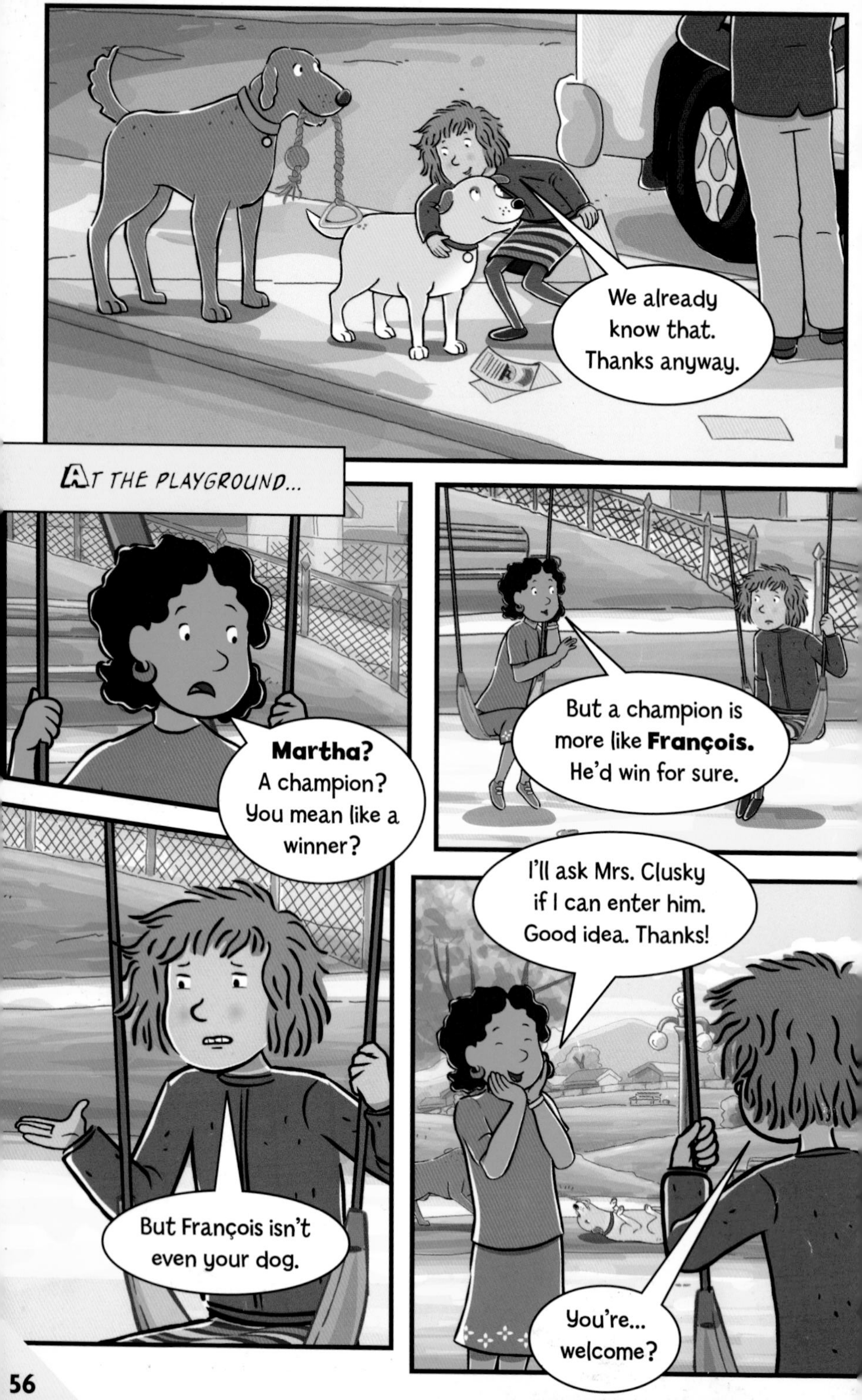
We already know that. Thanks anyway.
AT THE PLAYGROUND...
Martha? A champion? You mean like a winner?
But a champion is more like **François.** He'd win for sure.
But François isn't even your dog.
I'll ask Mrs. Clusky if I can enter him. Good idea. Thanks!
You're... welcome?

57

59

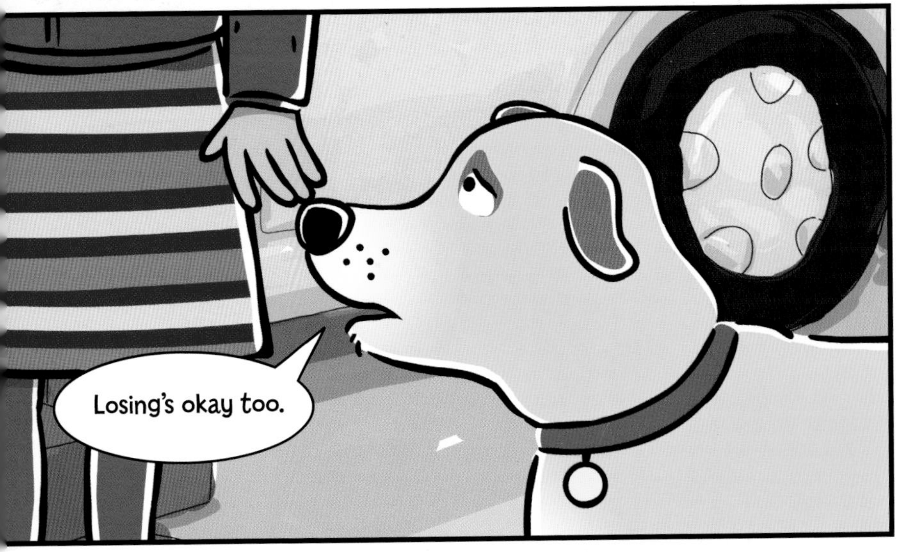
Losing's okay too.

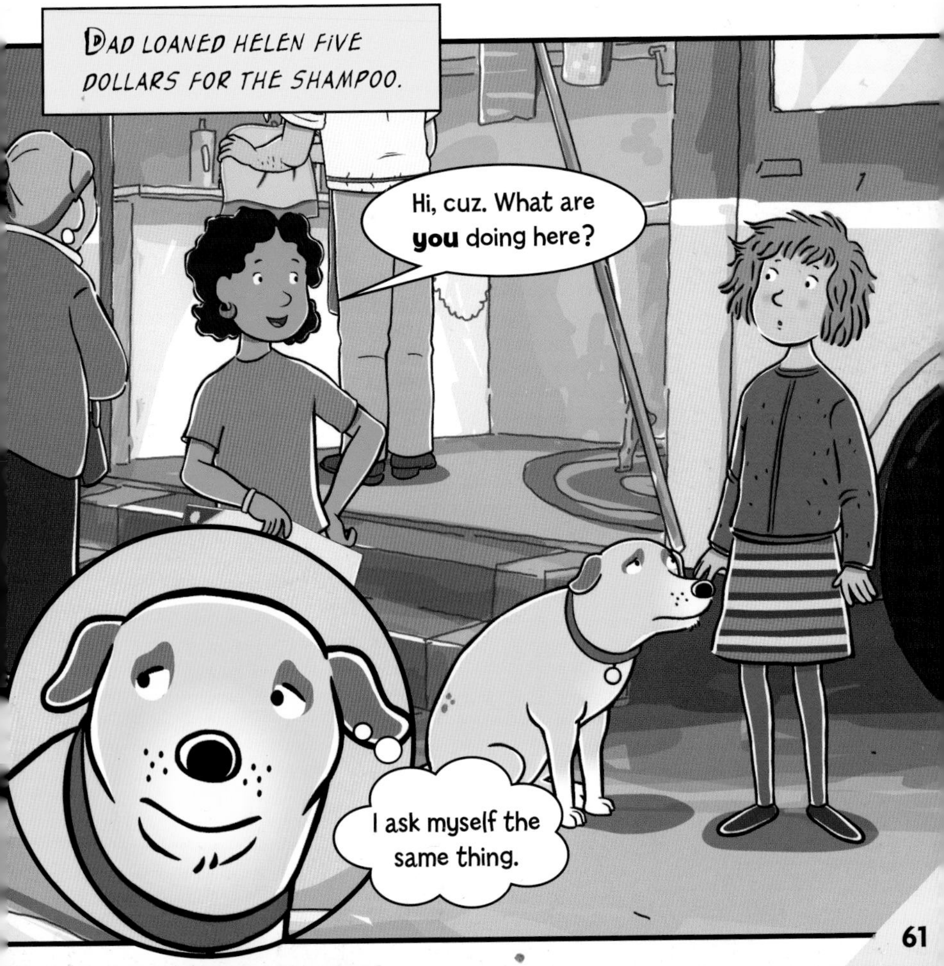
DAD LOANED HELEN FIVE DOLLARS FOR THE SHAMPOO.
Hi, cuz. What are **you** doing here?
I ask myself the same thing.

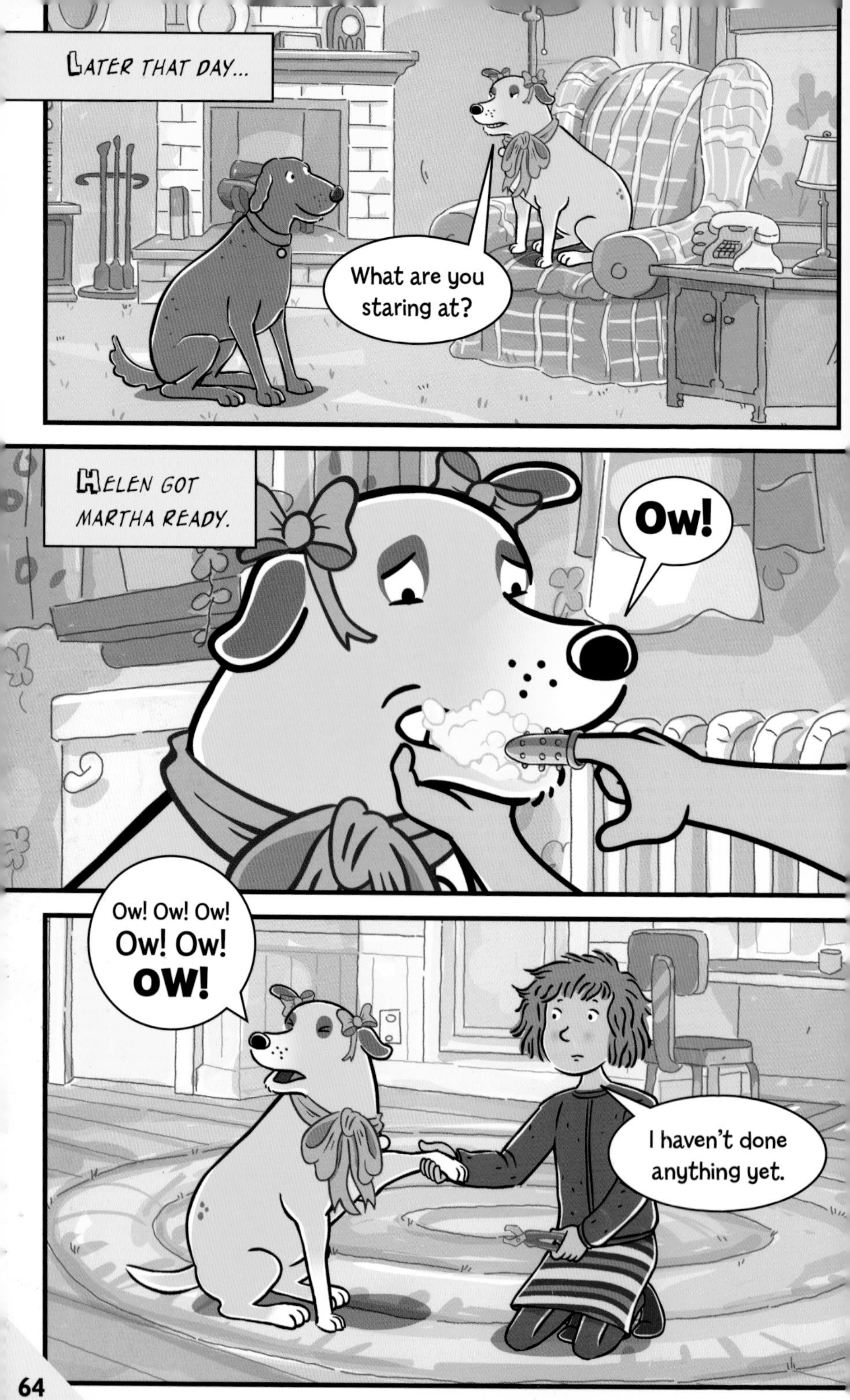
LATER THAT DAY...
What are you staring at?
HELEN GOT MARTHA READY.
Ow!
Ow! Ow! Ow! Ow! Ow! OW!
I haven't done anything yet.

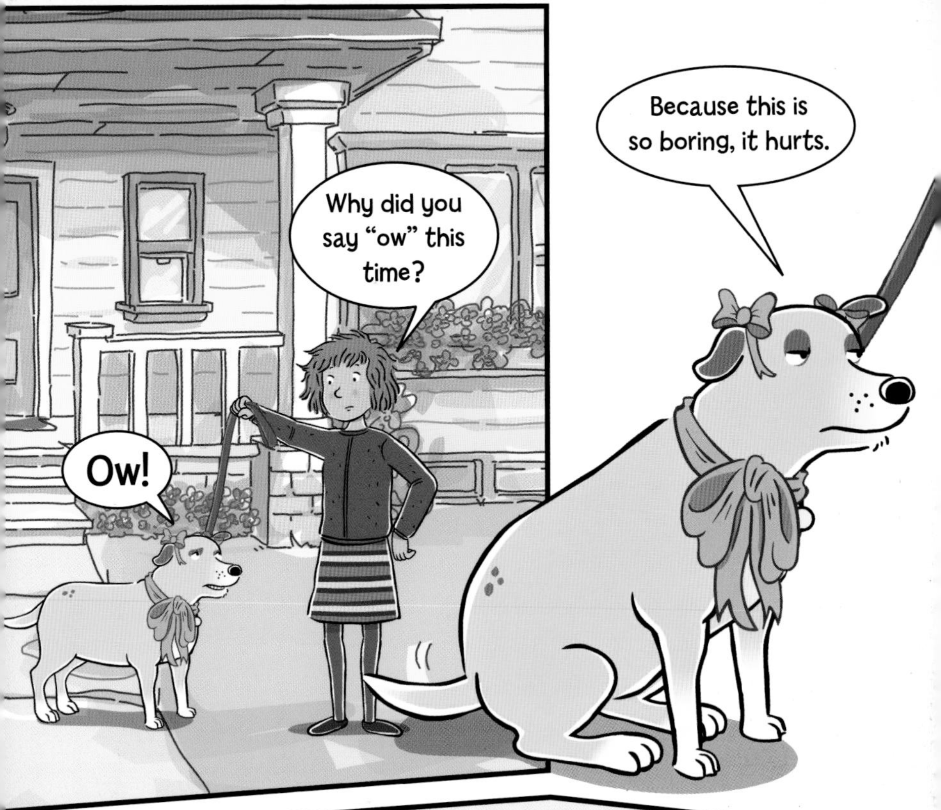
Ow!
Why did you say "ow" this time?
Because this is so boring, it hurts.

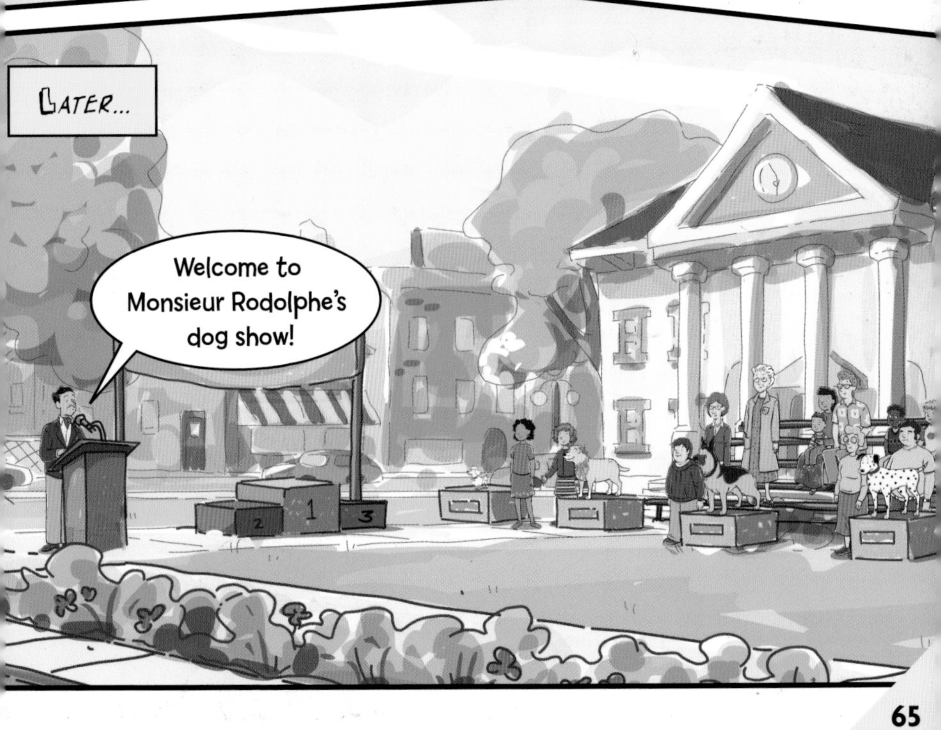
LATER...
Welcome to Monsieur Rodolphe's dog show!

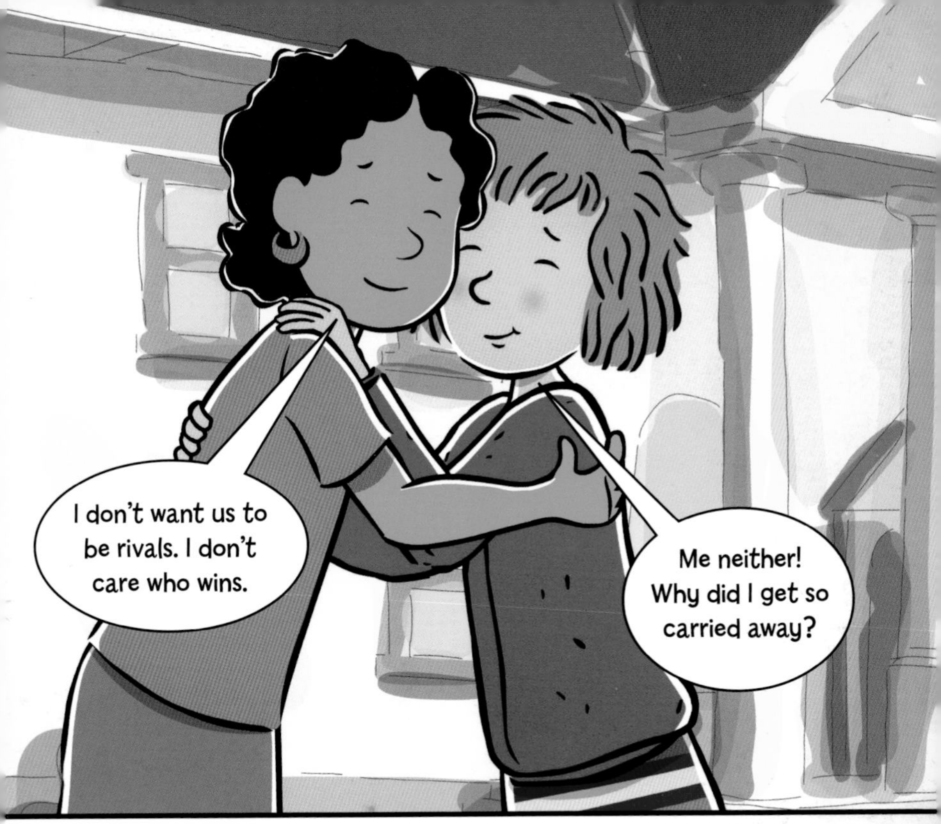
I don't want us to be rivals. I don't care who wins.
Me neither! Why did I get so carried away?

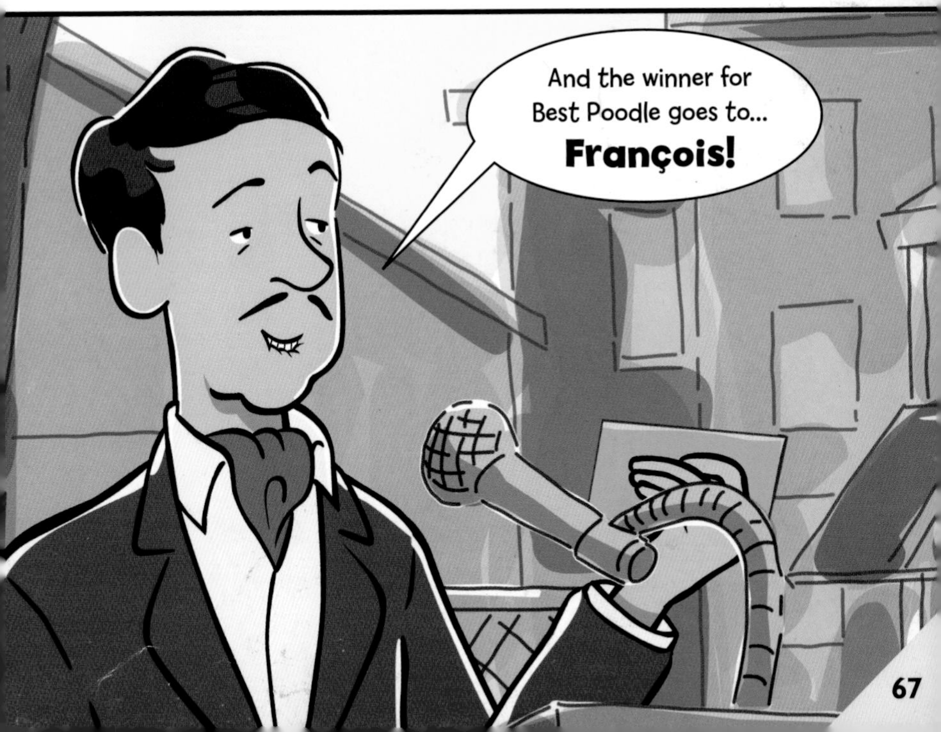
And the winner for Best Poodle goes to... **François!**

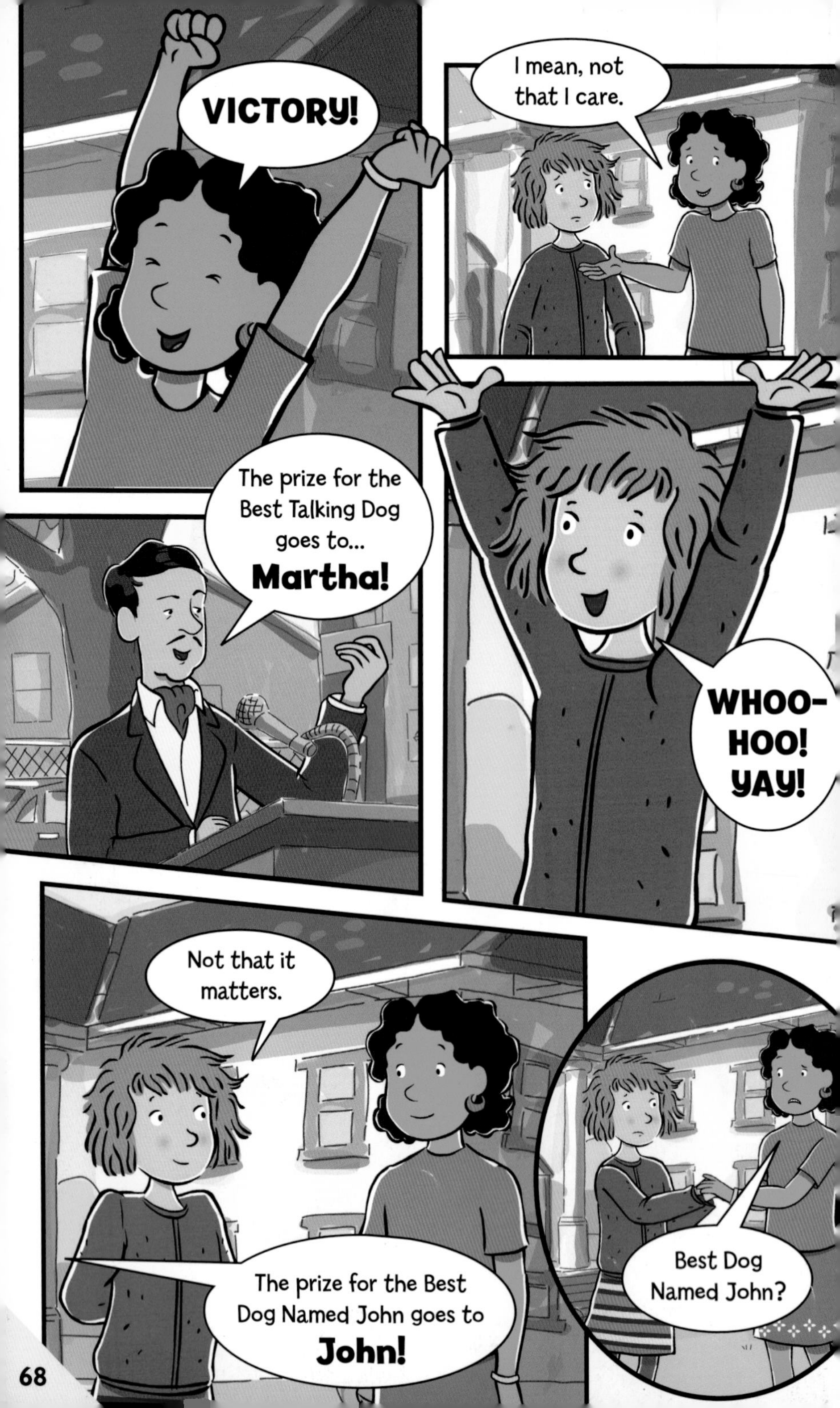
VICTORY!
I mean, not that I care.
The prize for the Best Talking Dog goes to... Martha!
WHOO-HOO! YAY!
Not that it matters.
The prize for the Best Dog Named John goes to John!
Best Dog Named John?

69

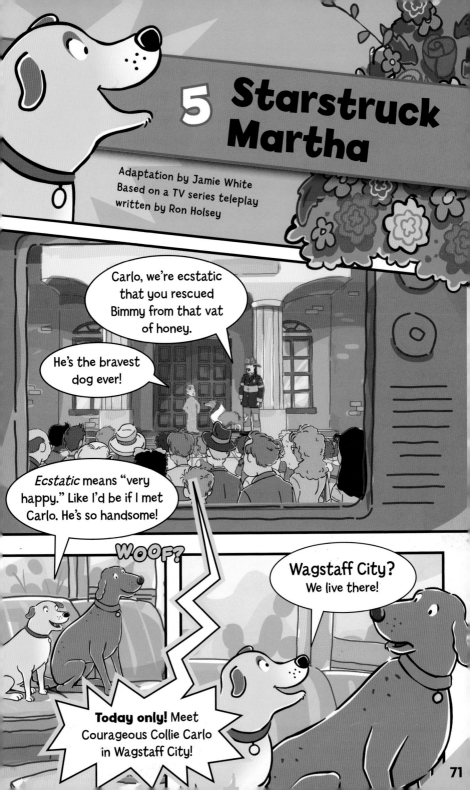

5 Starstruck Martha

Adaptation by Jamie White
Based on a TV series teleplay
written by Ron Holsey

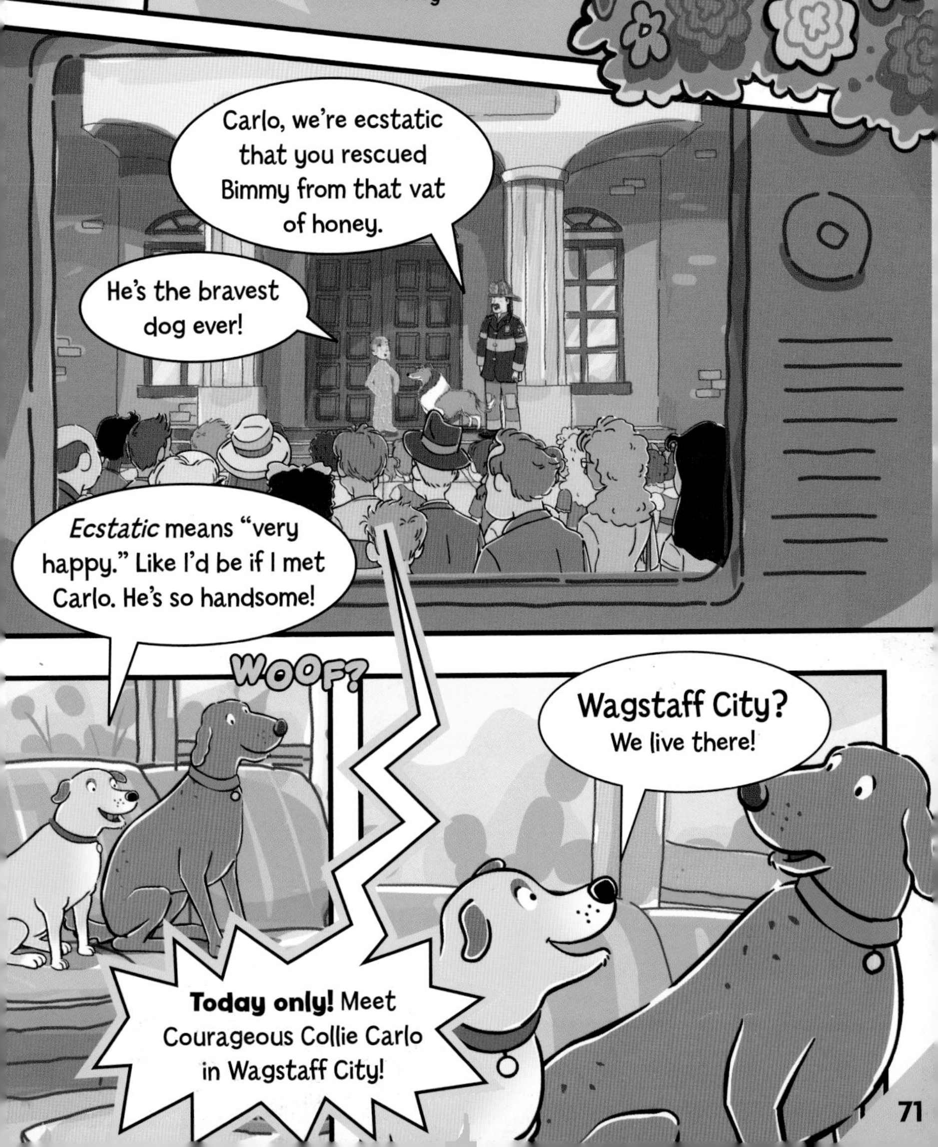

Carlo, we're ecstatic that you rescued Bimmy from that vat of honey.
He's the bravest dog ever!
Ecstatic means "very happy." Like I'd be if I met Carlo. He's so handsome!
WOOF?
Today only! Meet Courageous Collie Carlo in Wagstaff City!
Wagstaff City? We live there!

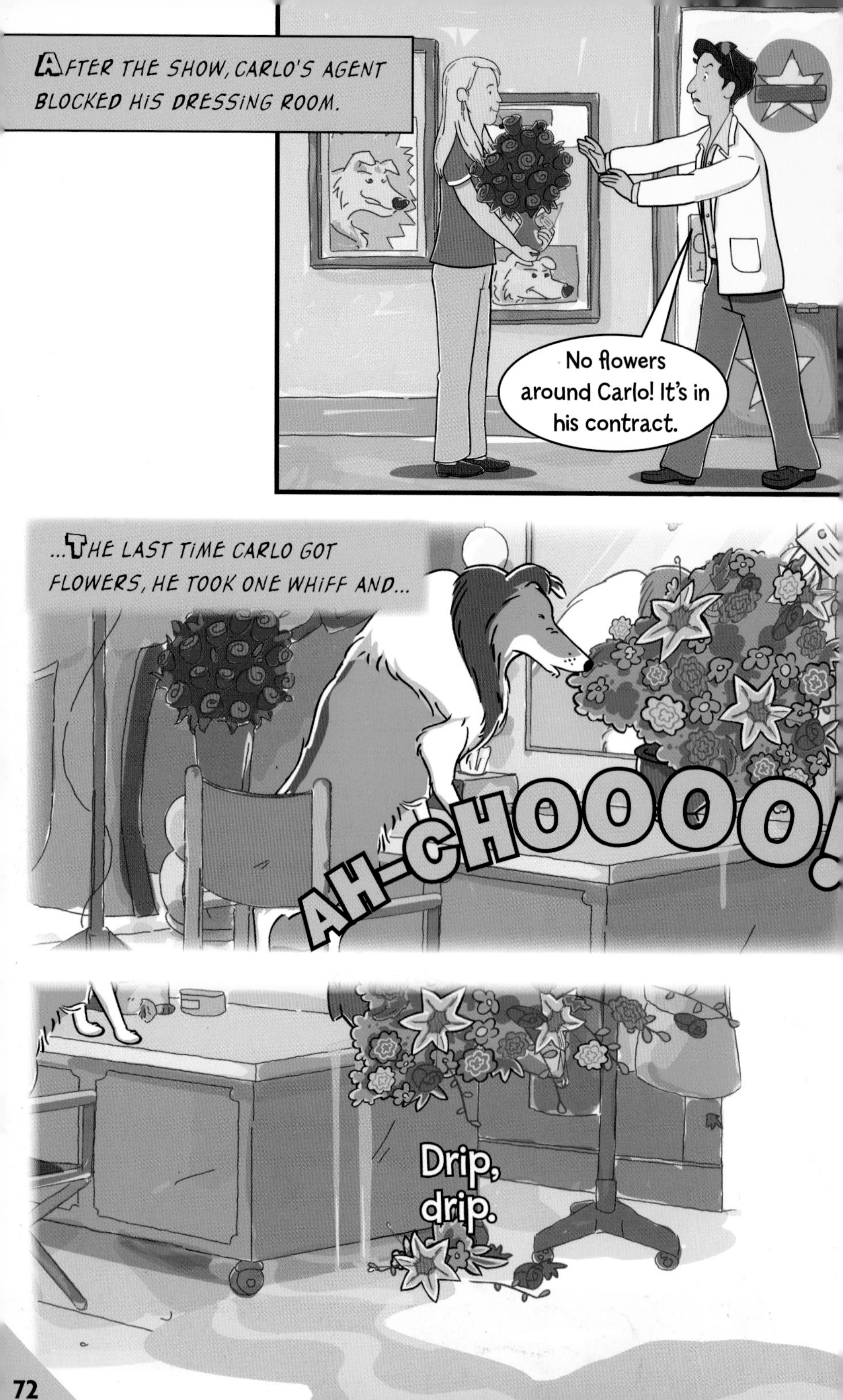
AFTER THE SHOW, CARLO'S AGENT BLOCKED HIS DRESSING ROOM.
No flowers around Carlo! It's in his contract.
...THE LAST TIME CARLO GOT FLOWERS, HE TOOK ONE WHIFF AND...
AH-CHOOOOO!
Drip, drip.

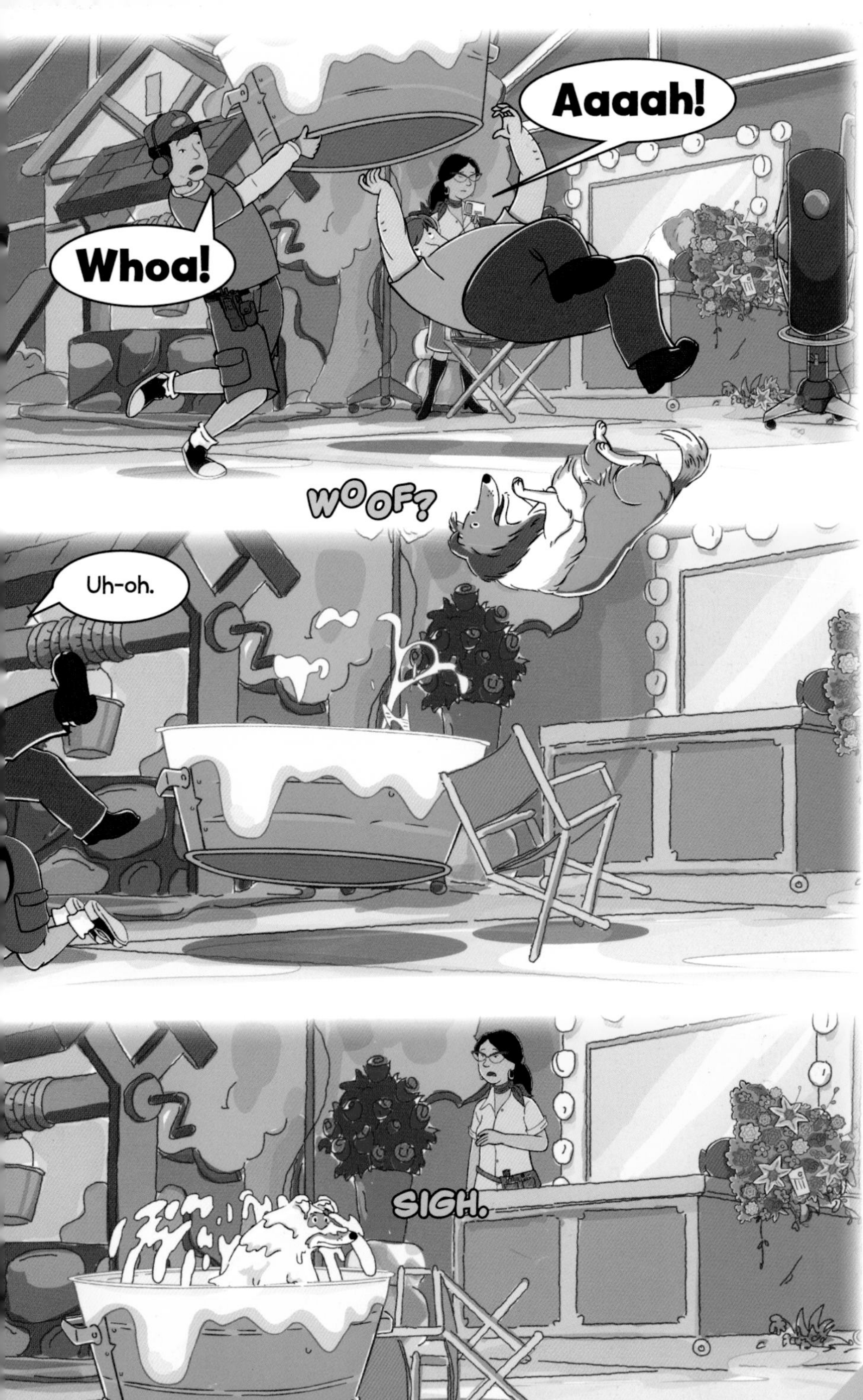
Aaaah!
Whoa!
WOOF?
Uh-oh.
SIGH.

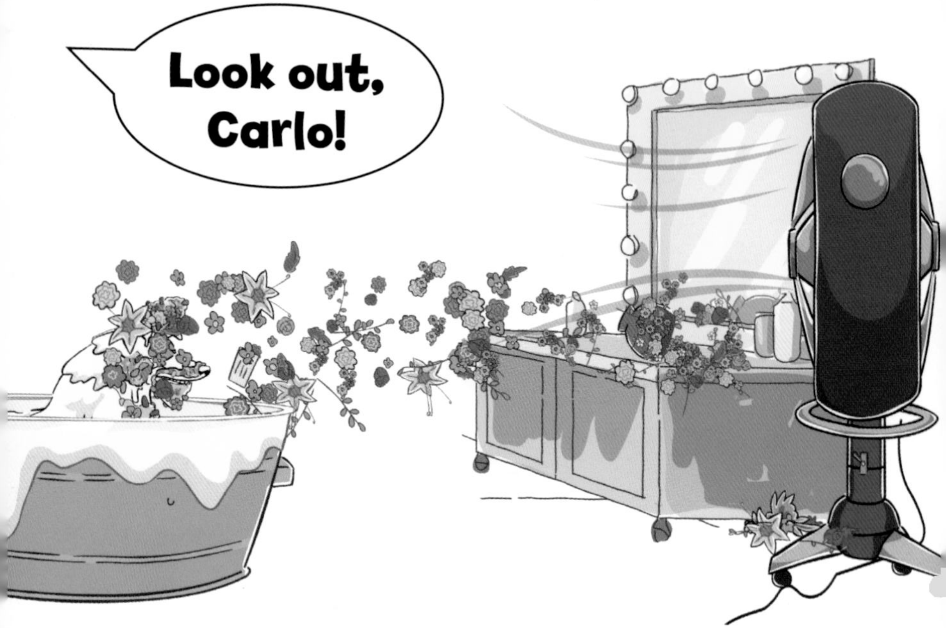
Look out, Carlo!

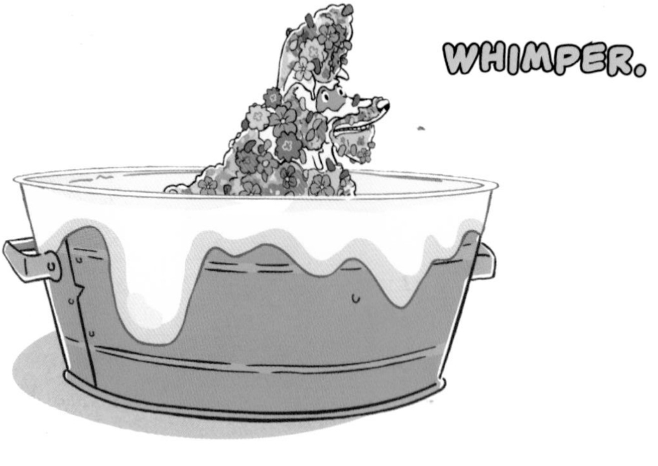
WHIMPER.

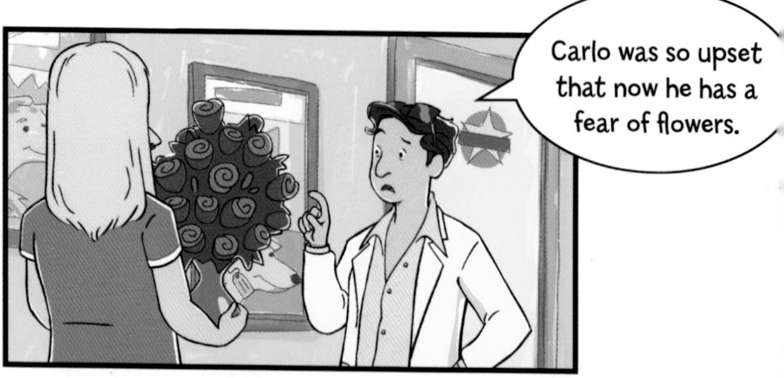
Carlo was so upset that now he has a fear of flowers.

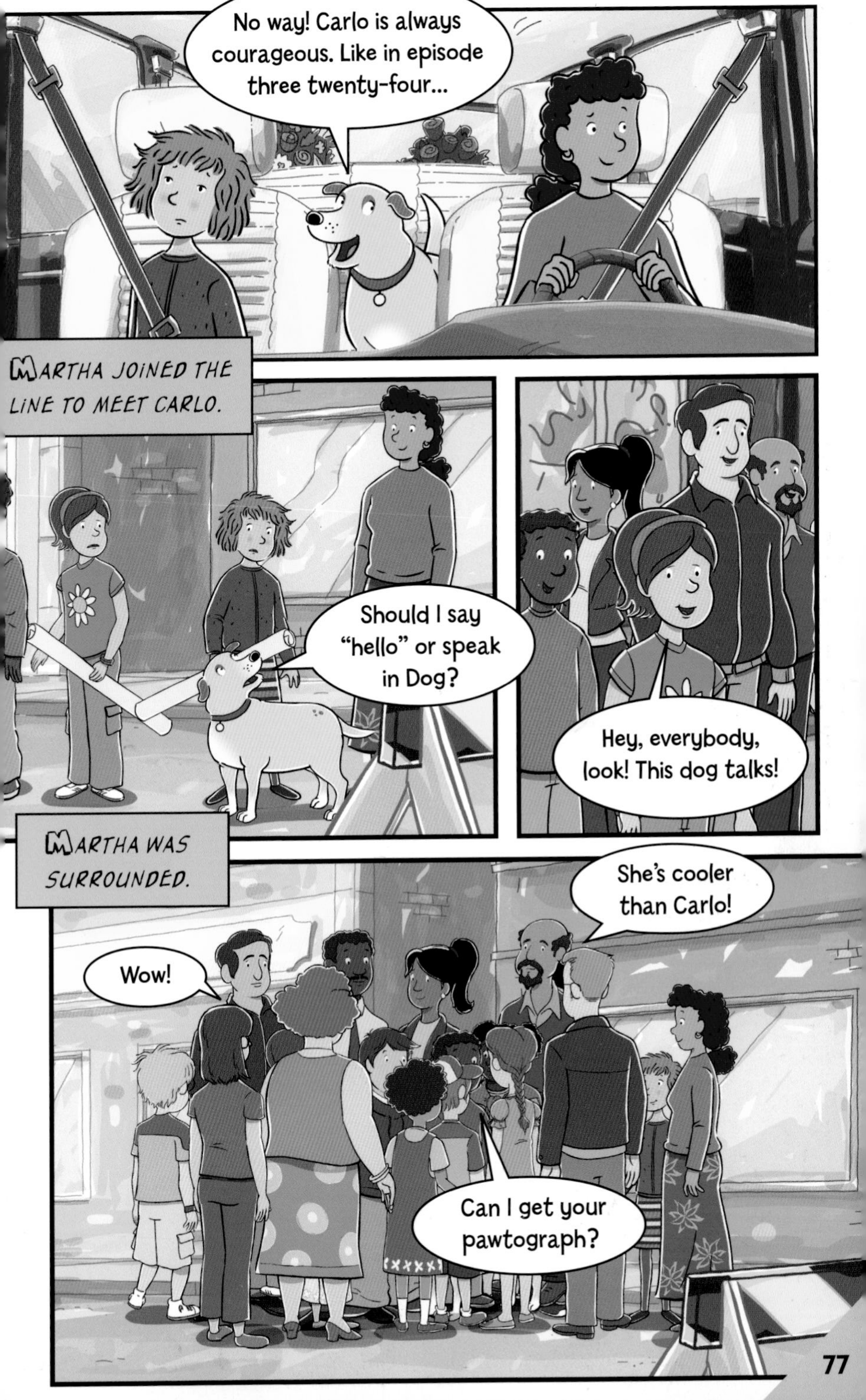
No way! Carlo is always courageous. Like in episode three twenty-four...
MARTHA JOINED THE LINE TO MEET CARLO.
Should I say "hello" or speak in Dog?
Hey, everybody, look! This dog talks!
MARTHA WAS SURROUNDED.
Wow!
She's cooler than Carlo!
Can I get your pawtograph?

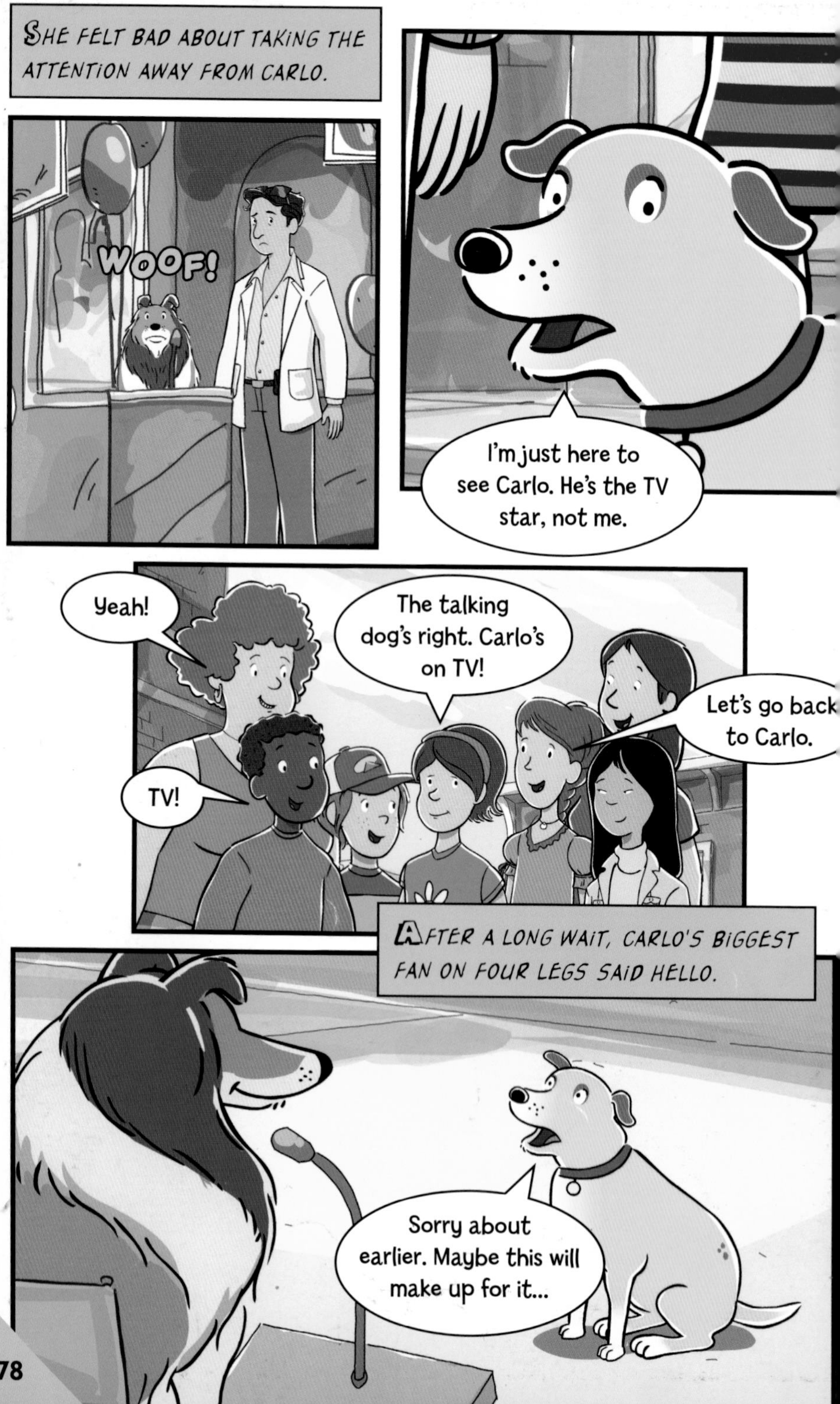
SHE FELT BAD ABOUT TAKING THE ATTENTION AWAY FROM CARLO.
WOOF!
I'm just here to see Carlo. He's the TV star, not me.
Yeah!
The talking dog's right. Carlo's on TV!
Let's go back to Carlo.
TV!
AFTER A LONG WAIT, CARLO'S BIGGEST FAN ON FOUR LEGS SAID HELLO.
Sorry about earlier. Maybe this will make up for it...

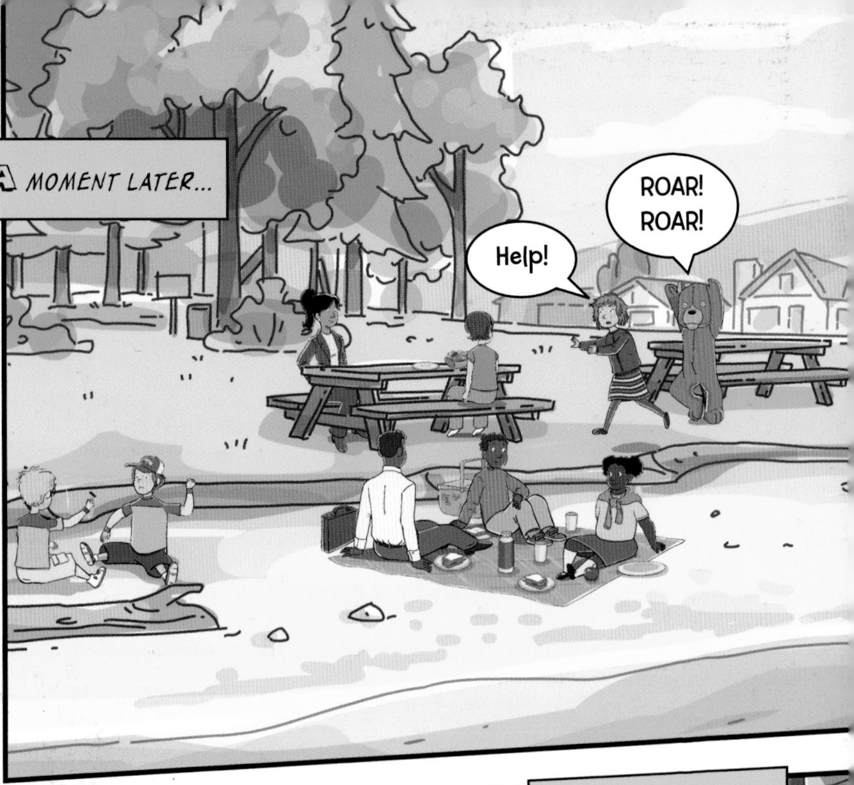
A MOMENT LATER...
Help!
ROAR! ROAR!

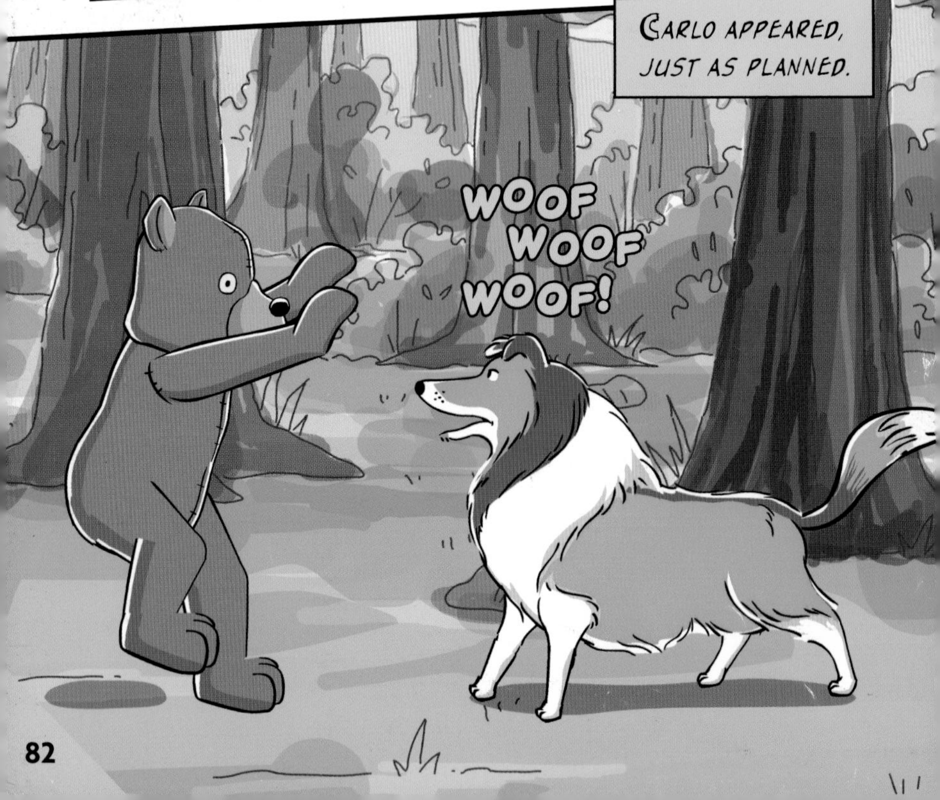
CARLO APPEARED, JUST AS PLANNED.
WOOF WOOF WOOF!

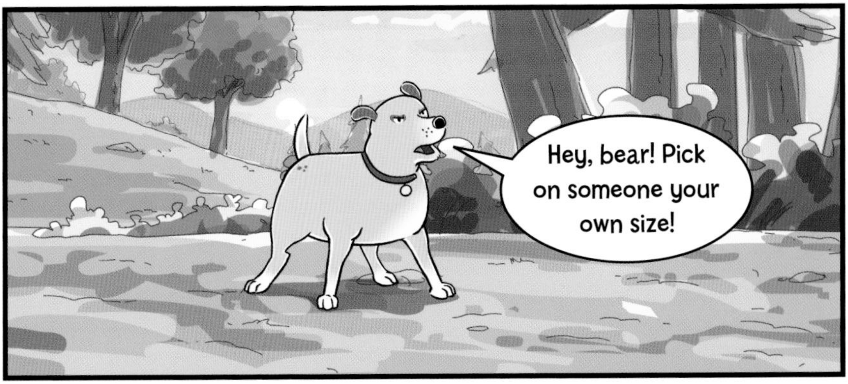
Hey, bear! Pick on someone your own size!

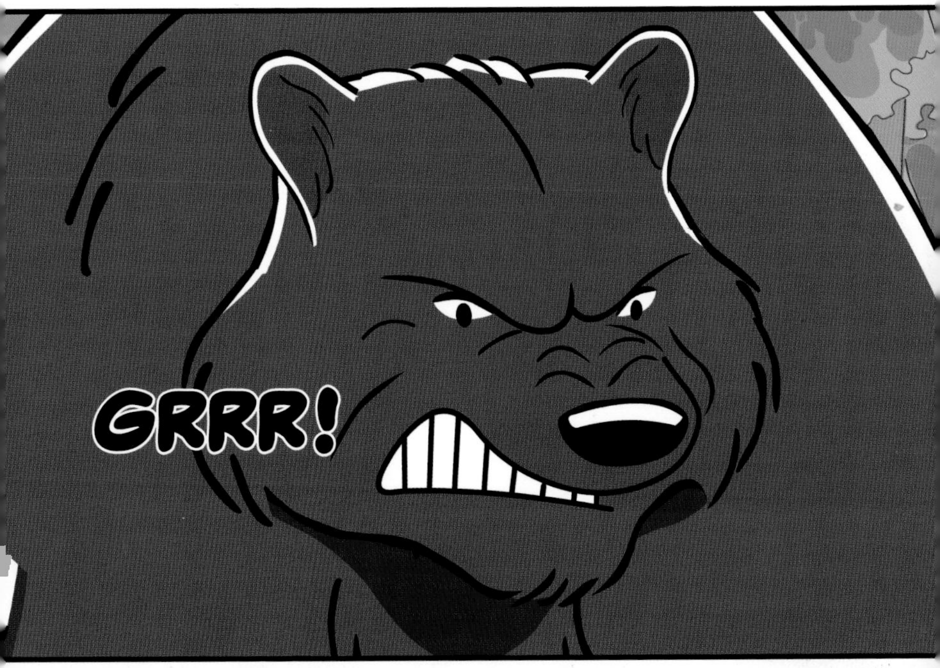
GRRR!

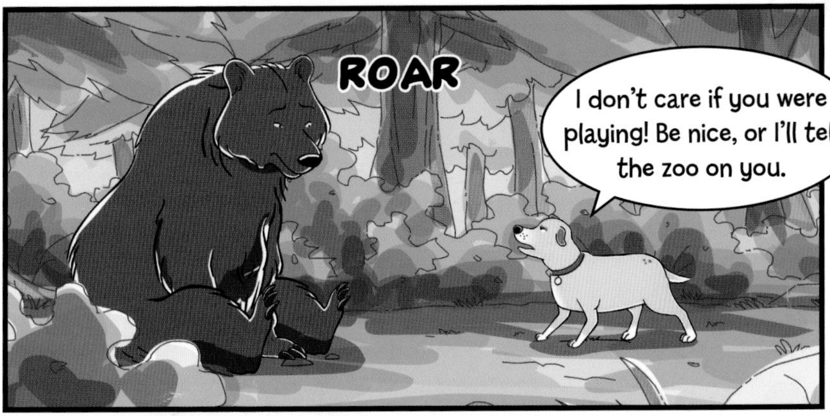
ROAR
I don't care if you were playing! Be nice, or I'll tell the zoo on you.

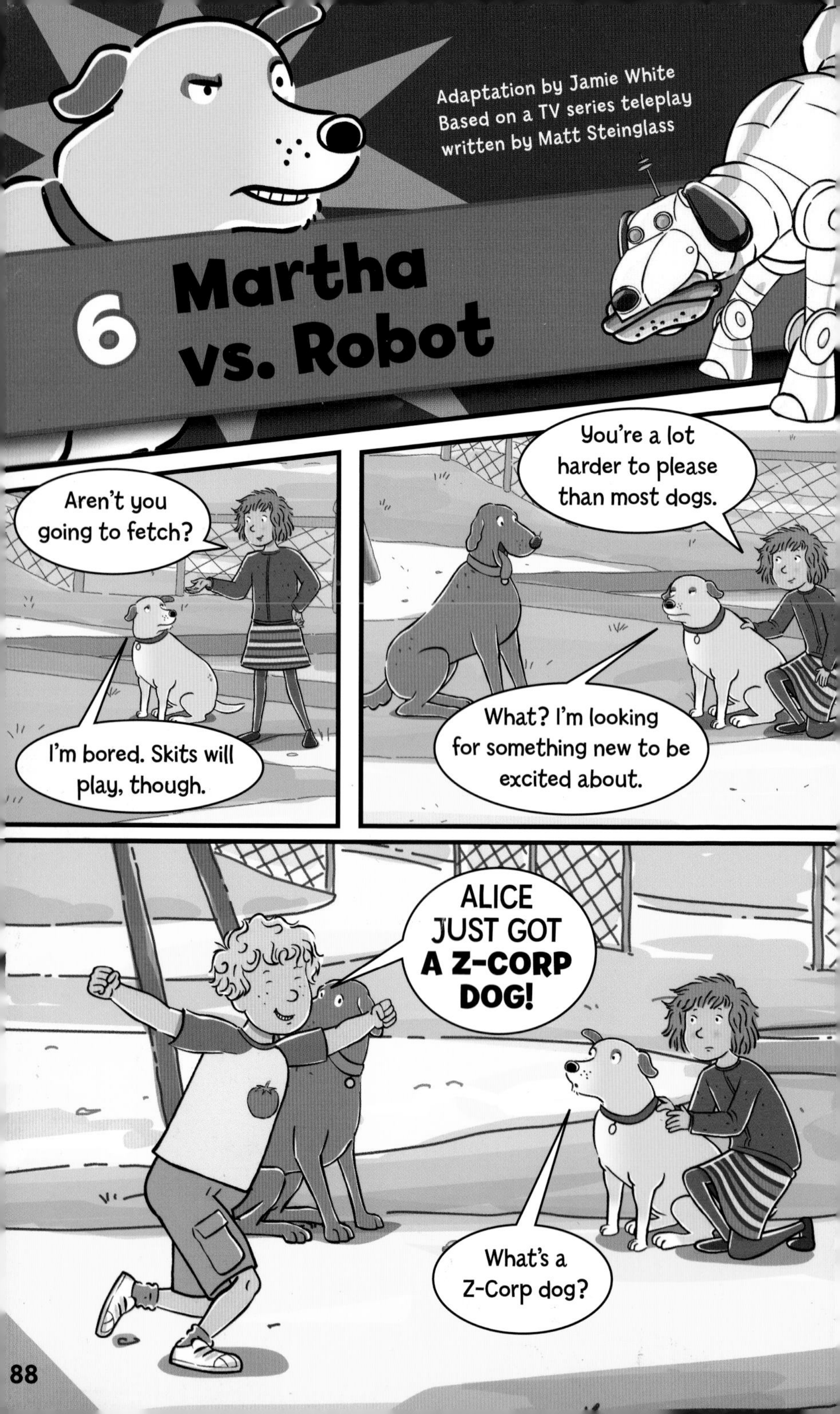
Adaptation by Jamie White
Based on a TV series teleplay
written by Matt Steinglass
6 Martha vs. Robot
Aren't you going to fetch?
I'm bored. Skits will play, though.
You're a lot harder to please than most dogs.
What? I'm looking for something new to be excited about.
ALICE JUST GOT **A Z-CORP DOG!**
What's a Z-Corp dog?

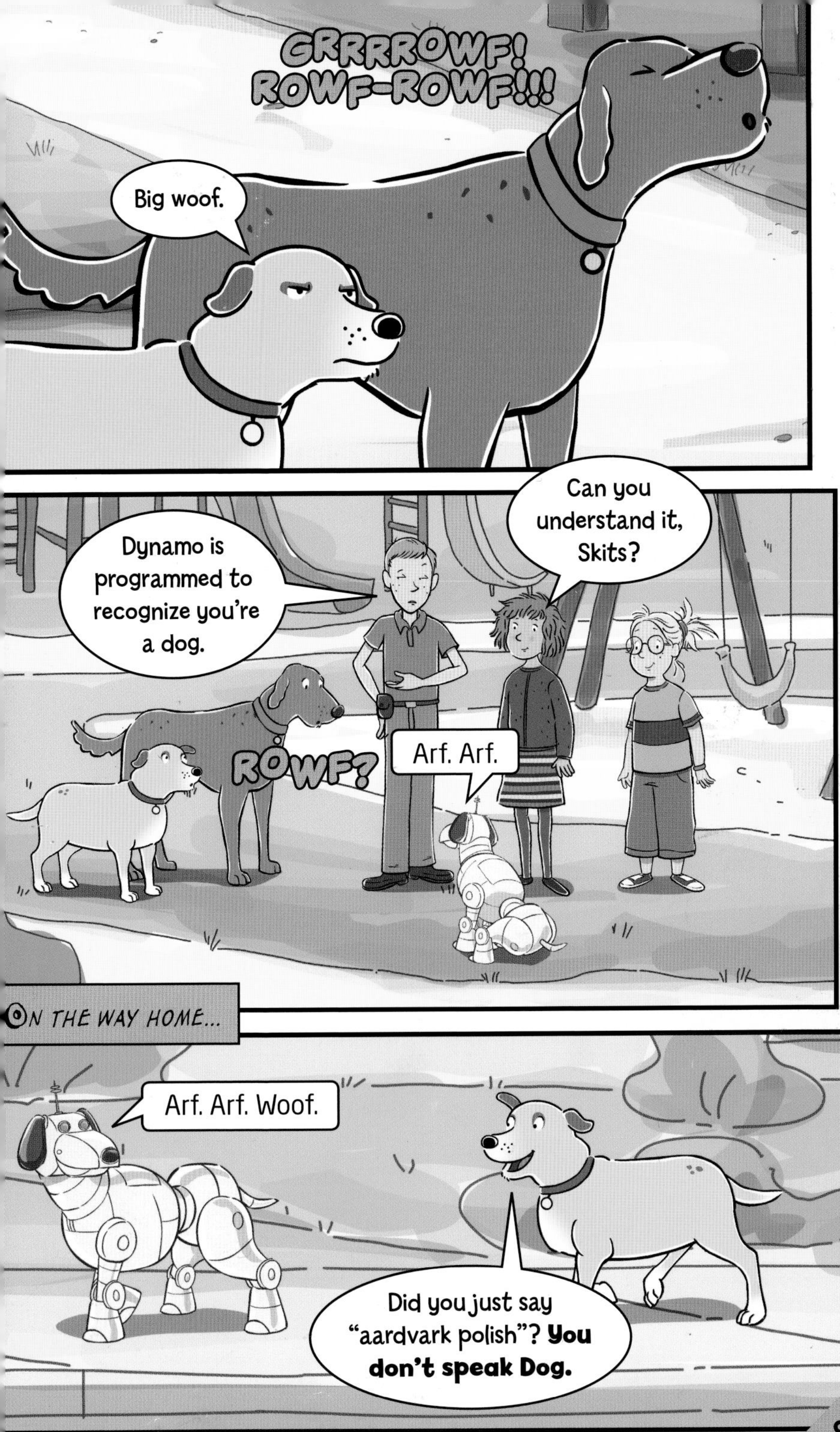

GRRRROWF! ROWF-ROWF!!!
Big woof.
Dynamo is programmed to recognize you're a dog.
Can you understand it, Skits?
ROWF?
Arf. Arf.
ON THE WAY HOME...
Arf. Arf. Woof.
Did you just say "aardvark polish"? **You don't speak Dog.**

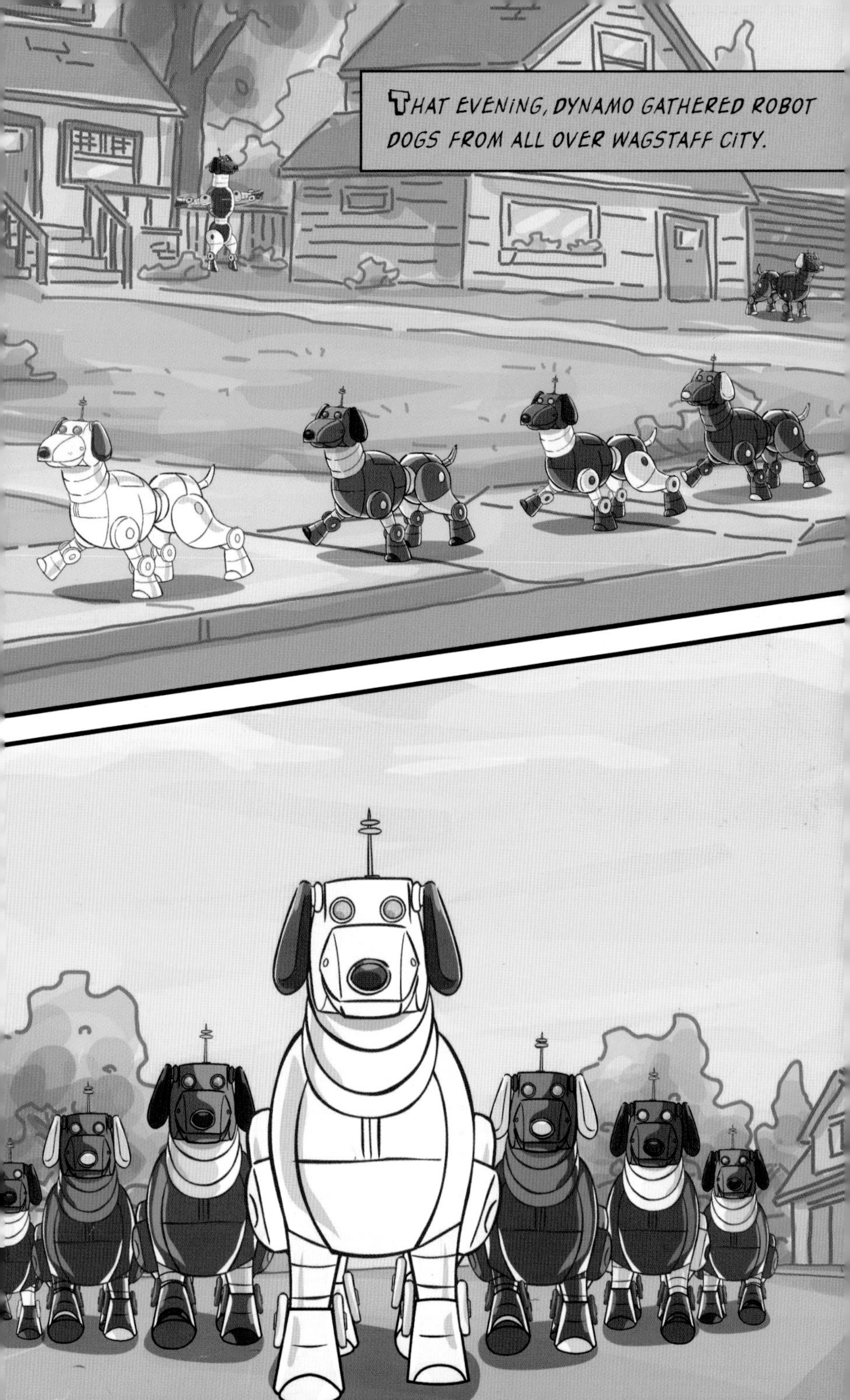
THAT EVENING, DYNAMO GATHERED ROBOT DOGS FROM ALL OVER WAGSTAFF CITY.

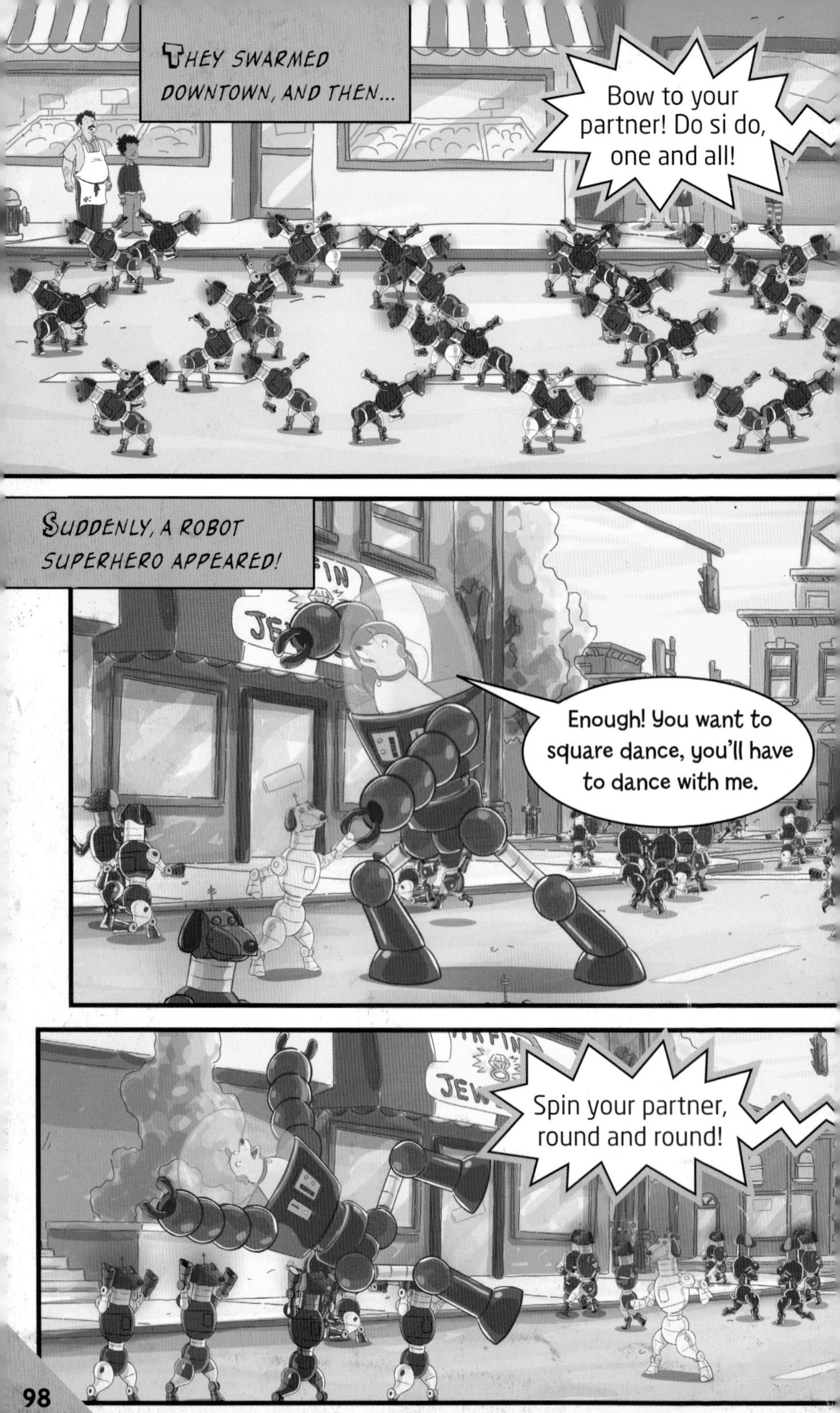
THEY SWARMED DOWNTOWN, AND THEN...
Bow to your partner! Do si do, one and all!
SUDDENLY, A ROBOT SUPERHERO APPEARED!
Enough! You want to square dance, you'll have to dance with me.
Spin your partner, round and round!

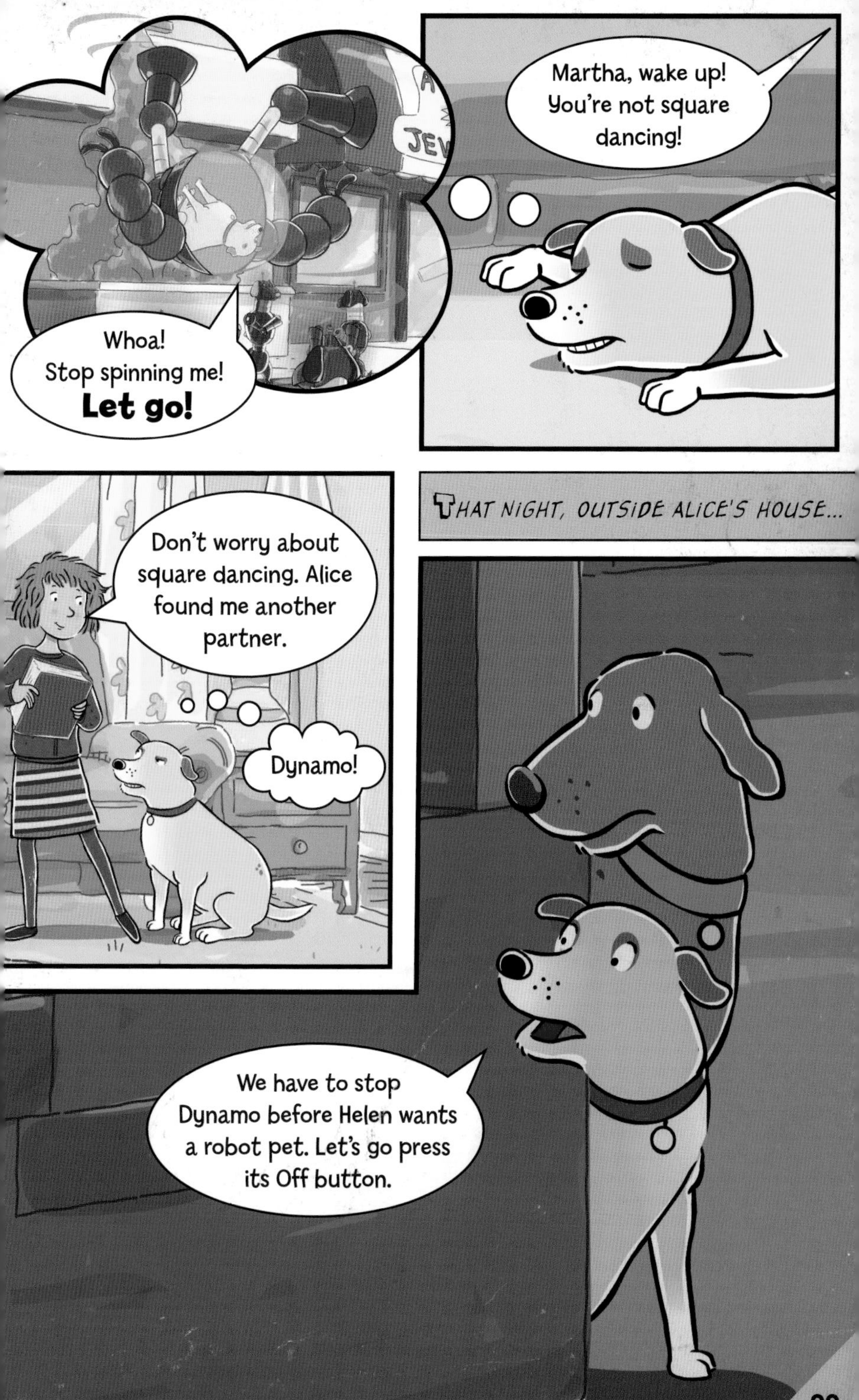
Whoa!
Stop spinning me!
Let go!
Martha, wake up! You're not square dancing!
Don't worry about square dancing. Alice found me another partner.
Dynamo!
THAT NIGHT, OUTSIDE ALICE'S HOUSE...
We have to stop Dynamo before Helen wants a robot pet. Let's go press its Off button.

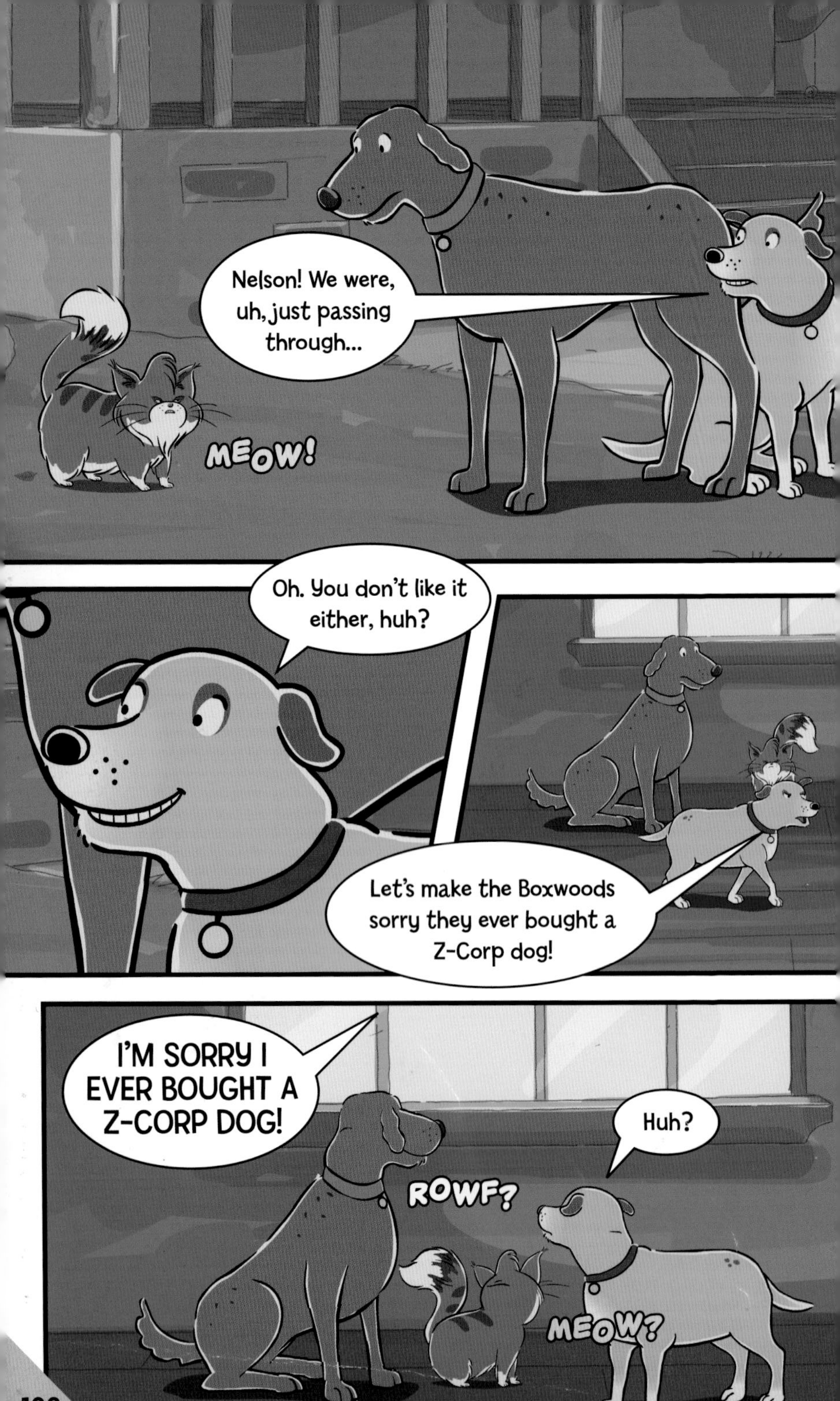
Nelson! We were, uh, just passing through...
MEOW!
Oh. You don't like it either, huh?
Let's make the Boxwoods sorry they ever bought a Z-Corp dog!
I'M SORRY I EVER BOUGHT A Z-CORP DOG!
Huh?
ROWF?
MEOW?

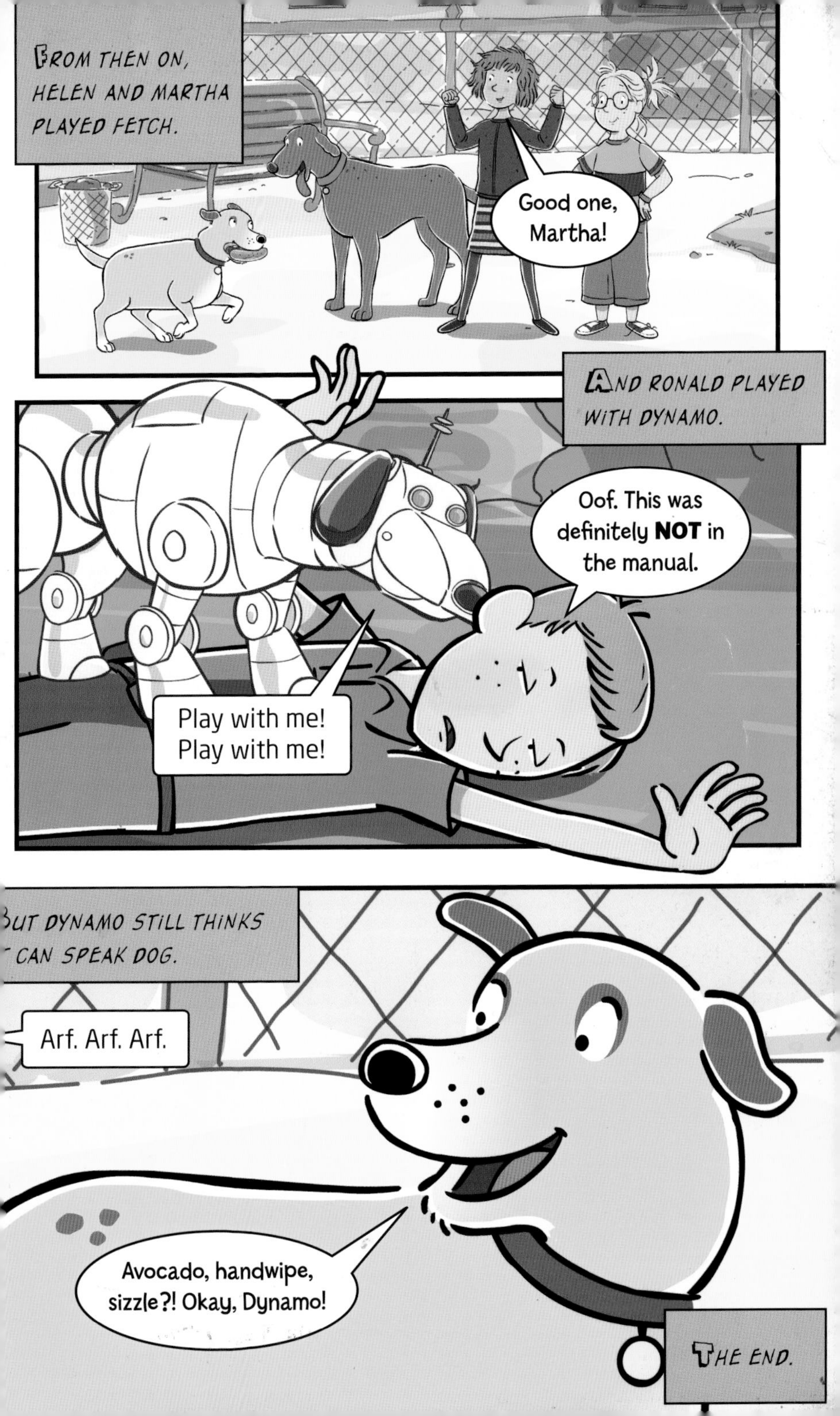
FROM THEN ON, HELEN AND MARTHA PLAYED FETCH.
Good one, Martha!
AND RONALD PLAYED WITH DYNAMO.
Oof. This was definitely **NOT** in the manual.
Play with me! Play with me!
UT DYNAMO STILL THINKS
CAN SPEAK DOG.
Arf. Arf. Arf.
Avocado, handwipe, sizzle?! Okay, Dynamo!
THE END.

A CANINE COMIC, STARRING YOU!

Imagine being on a neighborhood adventure with Martha and the dog pack. Create a comic book to tell your story.

Here's how:

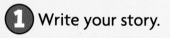

1 Write your story.

2 Practice drawing your characters.

3 Draw borders for each of your comic book panels. Panels are usually read in a Z pattern, so readers follow the action from left to right, diagonally left, and then right.

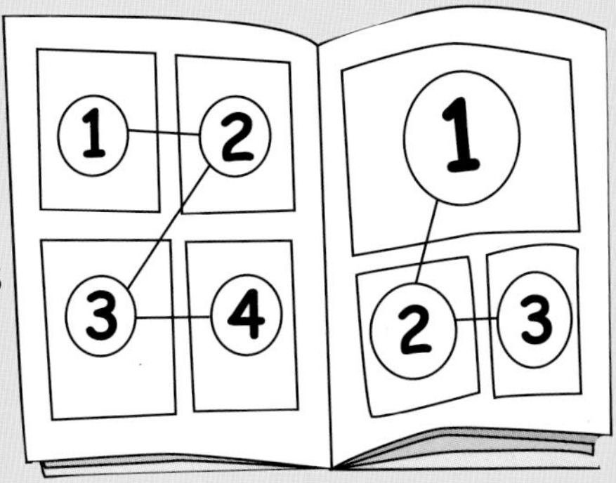
1
2
3
4
1
2
3

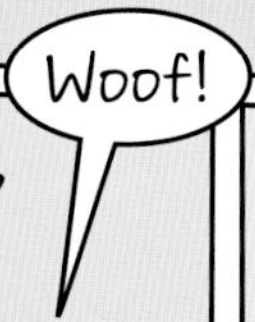
Woof!

4 Add speech bubbles, sound words, and other text. Make sure to leave room for the art.

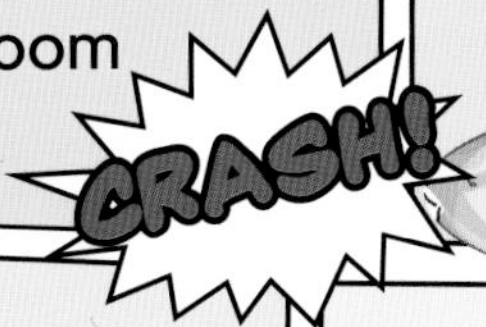
CRASH!

5 Sketch your drawings.

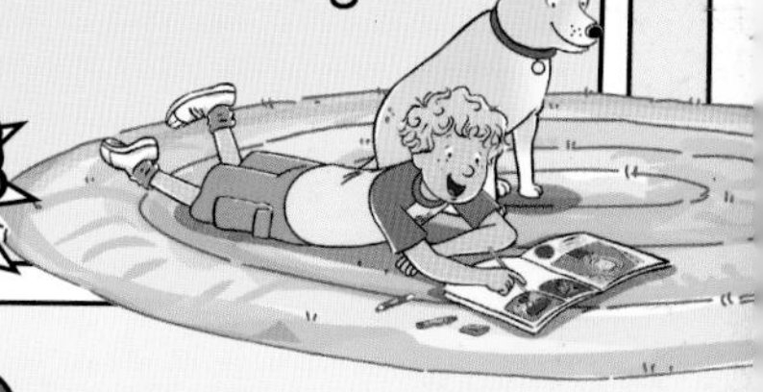

6 Trace the final sketches with ink. When the ink dries, erase your pencil lines.

7 Color the images.

8 When you're done, you can take your comic to a copy shop to have it printed.

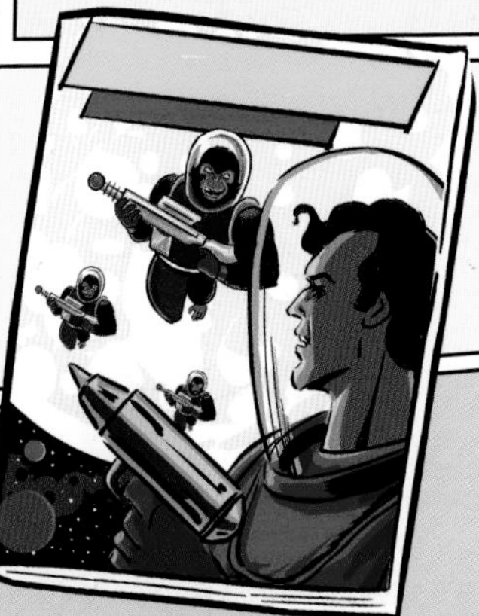

MARTHA'S STORY SQUARES

Stuck for ideas? Use Martha's Story Squares to spark an infinite number of comic book adventures. Close your eyes and drop your finger onto this page. Then see which square you've chosen. After picking five squares, create a comic that links together all five images. **Have fun!**

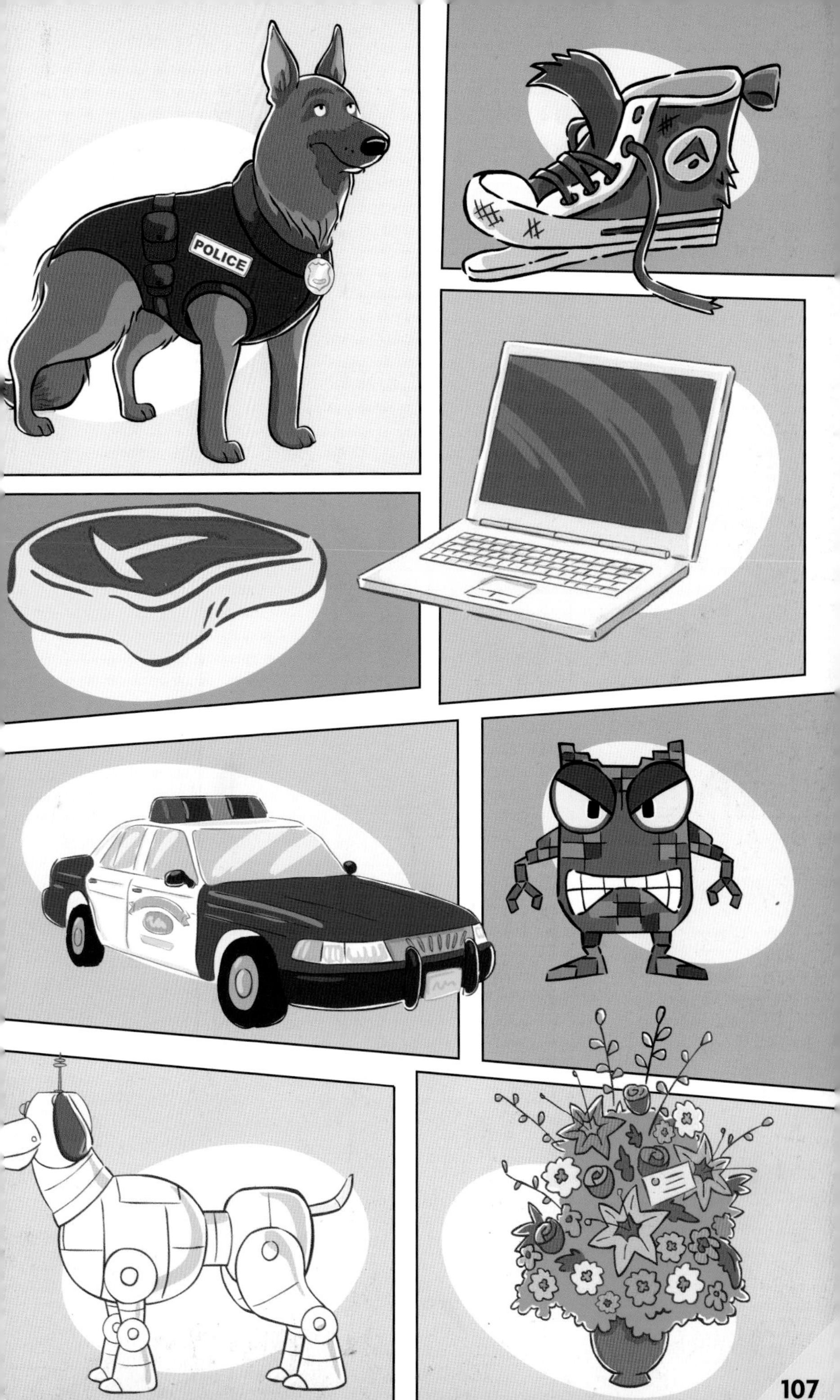
POLICE

DRAW DARING DOGS

Need some characters for your comic book adventure? Try tracing these canines! Place a sheet of thin drawing paper or tracing paper over the image you want to trace. Can you see the dog through your paper? Follow his or her outline with your pencil, and voila!

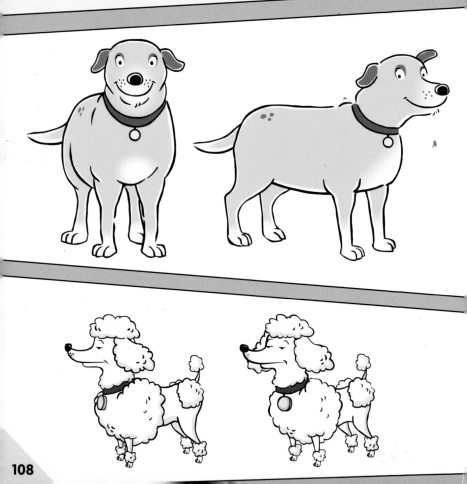

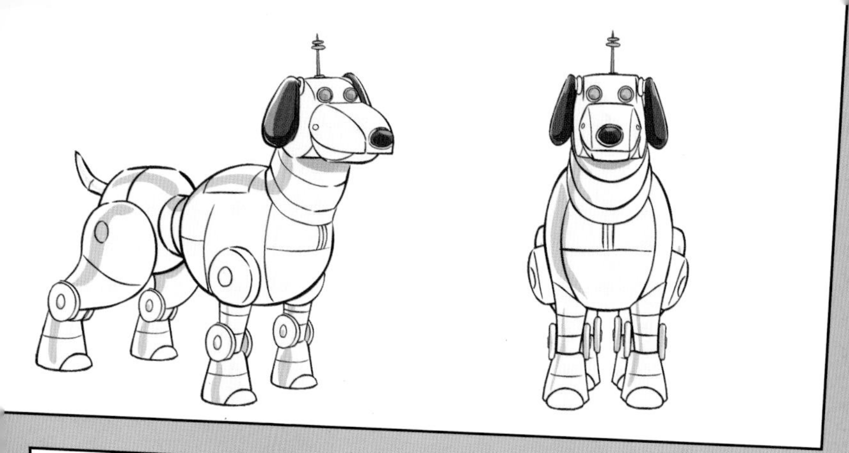

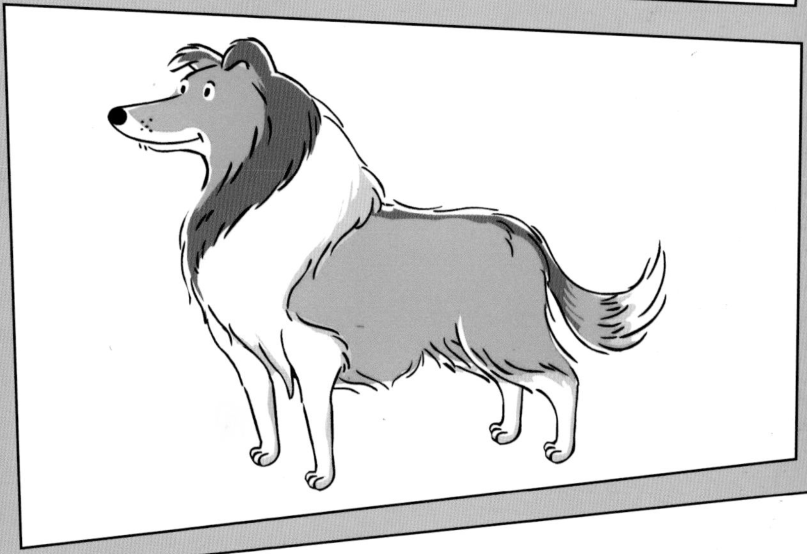

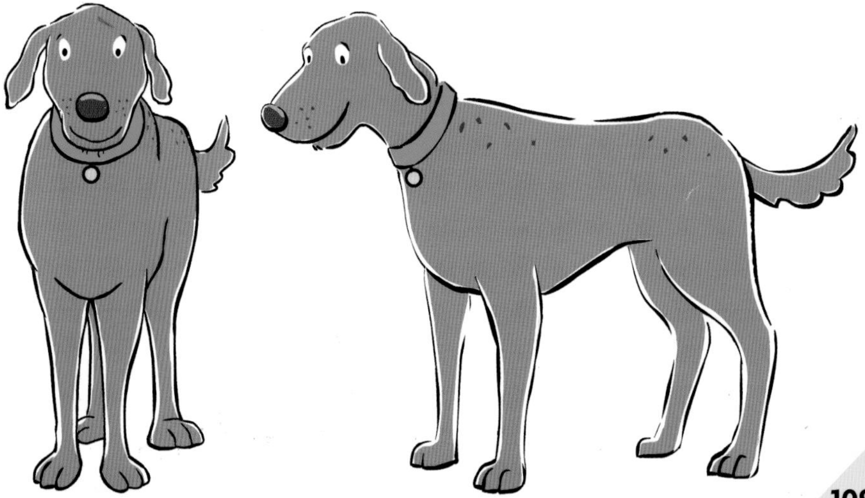

Be sure to check out all of these MARTHA SPEAKS adventures!

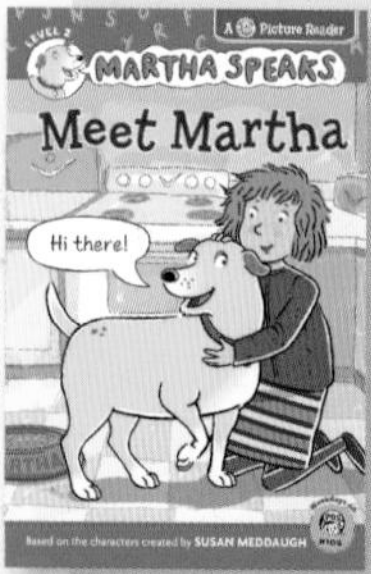
A Picture Reader
LEVEL 2
MARTHA SPEAKS
Meet Martha
Hi there!
Based on the characters created by SUSAN MEDDAUGH

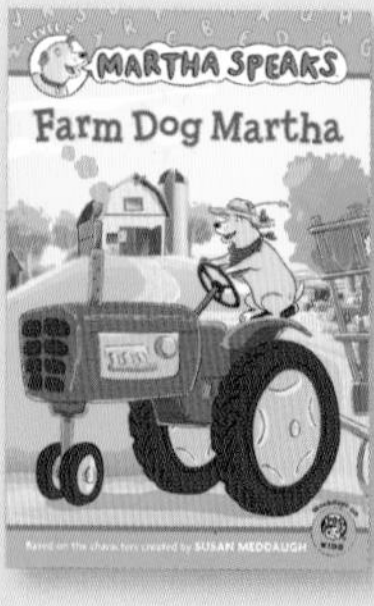
MARTHA SPEAKS
Farm Dog Martha
Based on the characters created by SUSAN MEDDAUGH

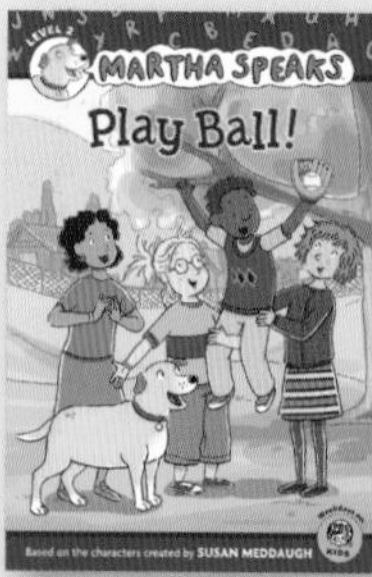
LEVEL 2
MARTHA SPEAKS
Play Ball!
Based on the characters created by SUSAN MEDDAUGH

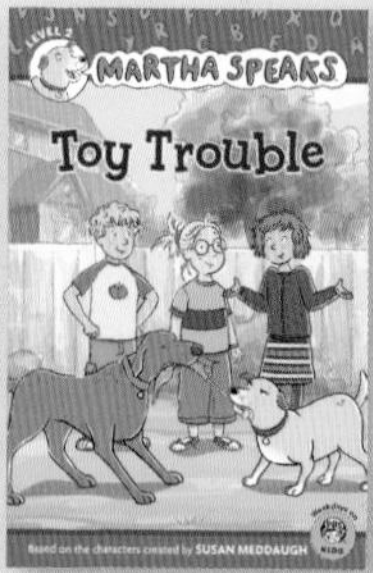
MARTHA SPEAKS
Toy Trouble
Based on the characters created by SUSAN MEDDAUGH

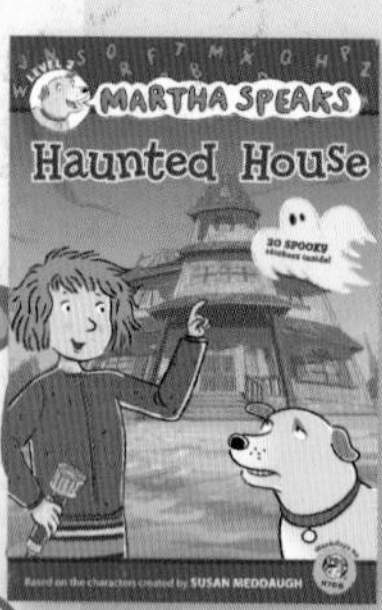
LEVEL 2
MARTHA SPEAKS
Haunted House
Based on the characters created by SUSAN MEDDAUGH

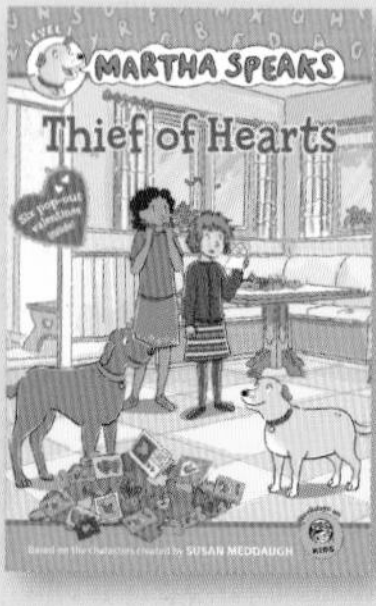
MARTHA SPEAKS
Thief of Hearts
Based on the characters created by SUSAN MEDDAUGH

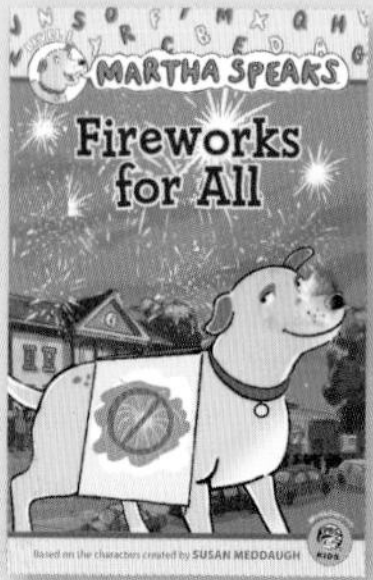
MARTHA SPEAKS
Fireworks for All
Based on the characters created by SUSAN MEDDAUGH

Now available in Spanish bilingual!

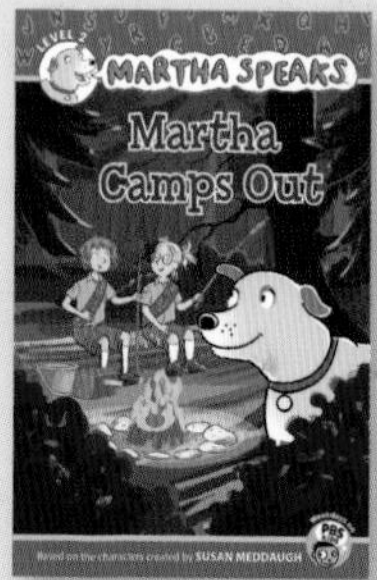
MARTHA SPEAKS
Martha Camps Out
Based on the characters created by SUSAN MEDDAUGH

Now available in Spanish bilingual!

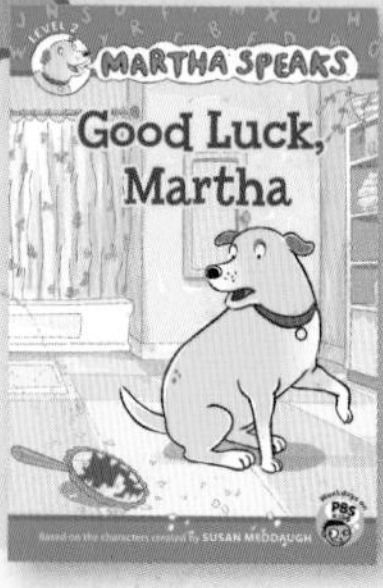
LEVEL 2
MARTHA SPEAKS
Good Luck, Martha
Based on the characters created by SUSAN MEDDAUGH

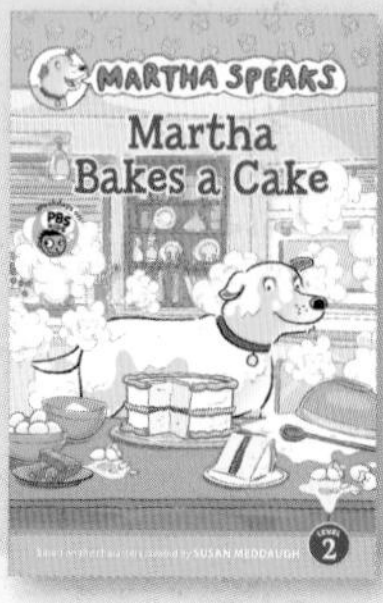
MARTHA SPEAKS
Martha Bakes a Cake
2

Now available in Spanish bilingual!

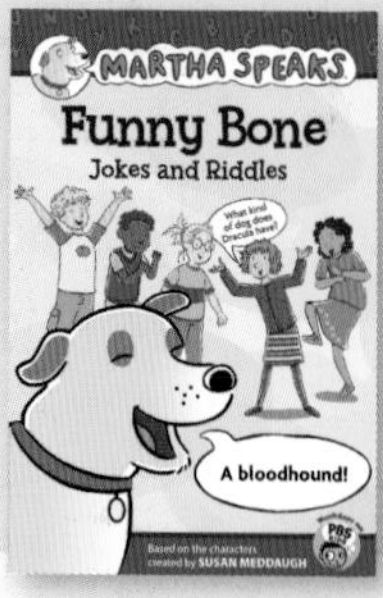
MARTHA SPEAKS
Funny Bone
Jokes and Riddles
A bloodhound!
Based on the characters created by SUSAN MEDDAUGH

Early readers

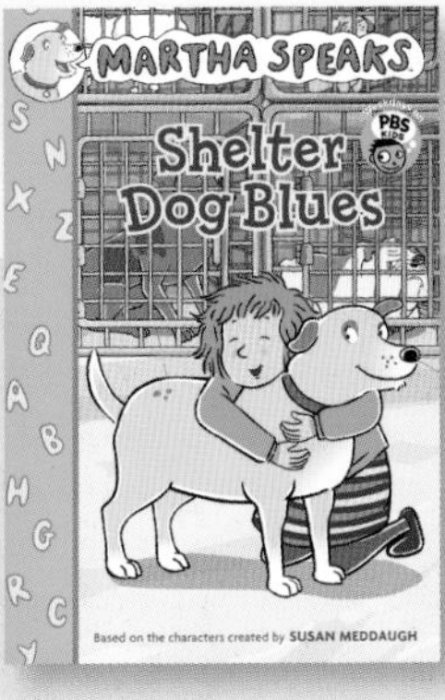
MARTHA SPEAKS
Shelter Dog Blues
PBS KIDS
Based on the characters created by SUSAN MEDDAUGH
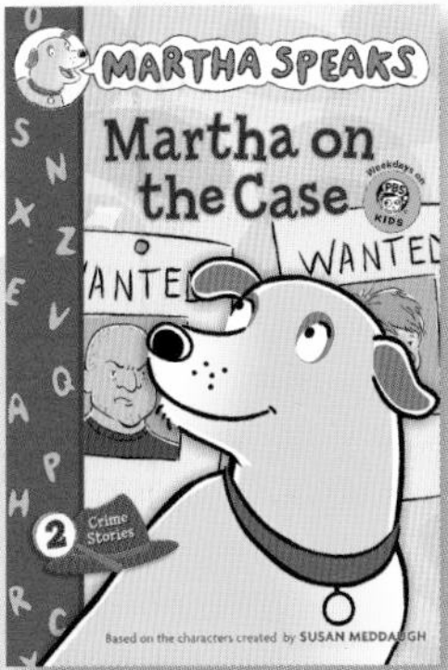
MARTHA SPEAKS
Martha on the Case
Weekdays on PBS KIDS
WANTED
2 Crime Stories
Based on the characters created by SUSAN MEDDAUGH
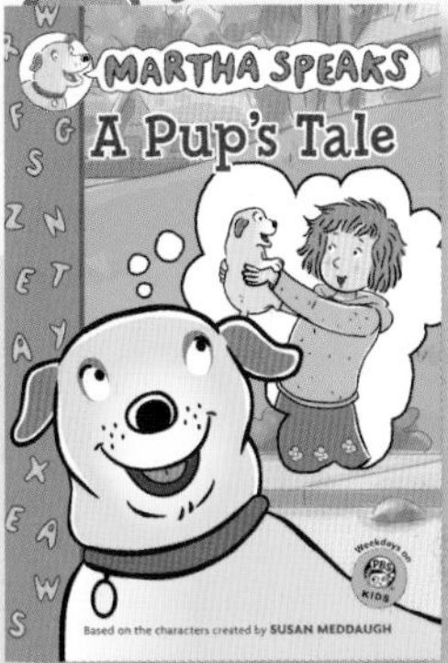
MARTHA SPEAKS
A Pup's Tale
Weekdays on PBS KIDS
Based on the characters created by SUSAN MEDDAUGH
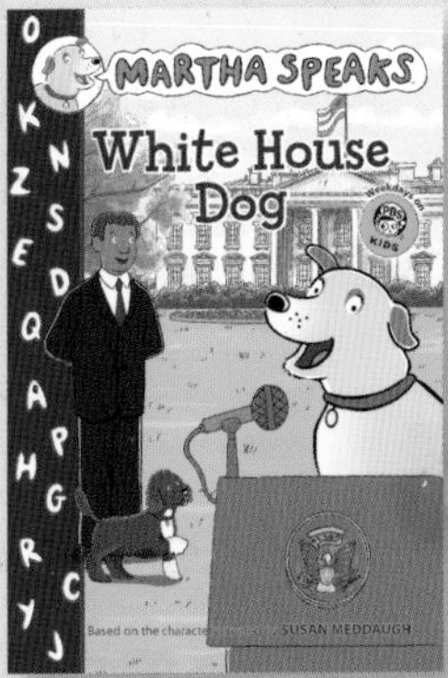
MARTHA SPEAKS
White House Dog
Weekdays on PBS KIDS
SUSAN MEDDAUGH
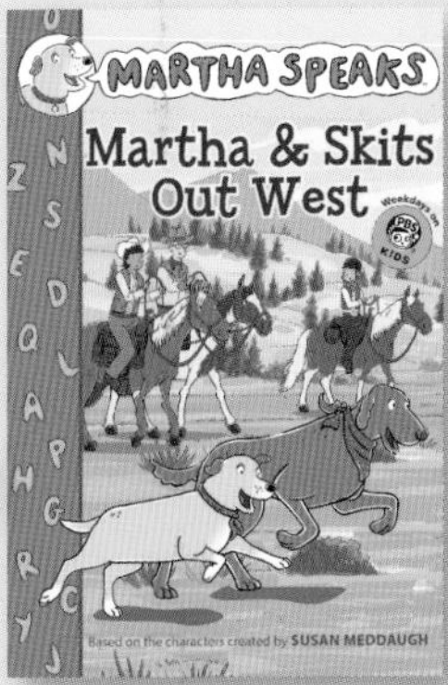
MARTHA SPEAKS
Martha & Skits Out West
Weekdays on PBS KIDS
Based on the characters created by SUSAN MEDDAUGH
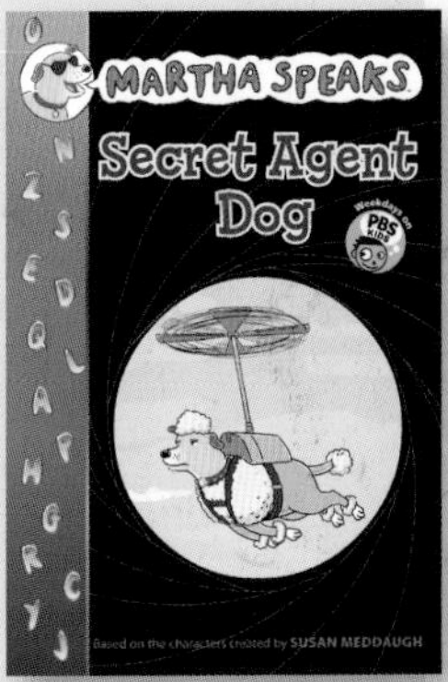
MARTHA SPEAKS
Secret Agent Dog
Weekdays on PBS KIDS
Based on the characters created by SUSAN MEDDAUGH
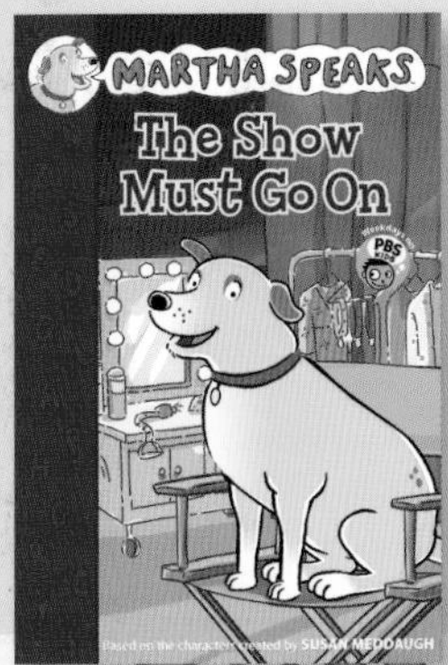
MARTHA SPEAKS
The Show Must Go On
Weekdays on PBS KIDS
Based on the characters created by SUSAN MEDDAUGH
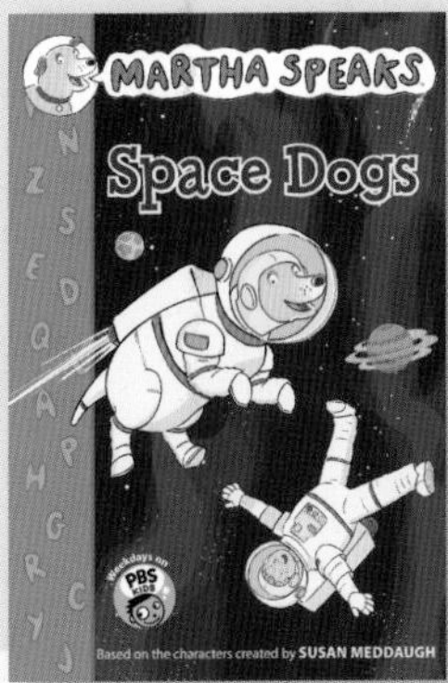
MARTHA SPEAKS
Space Dogs
Weekdays on PBS KIDS
Based on the characters created by SUSAN MEDDAUGH
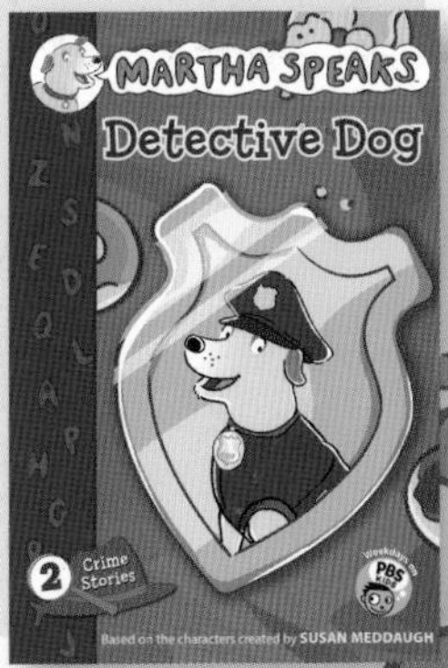
MARTHA SPEAKS
Detective Dog
2 Crime Stories
Weekdays on PBS KIDS
Based on the characters created by SUSAN MEDDAUGH

Chapter books

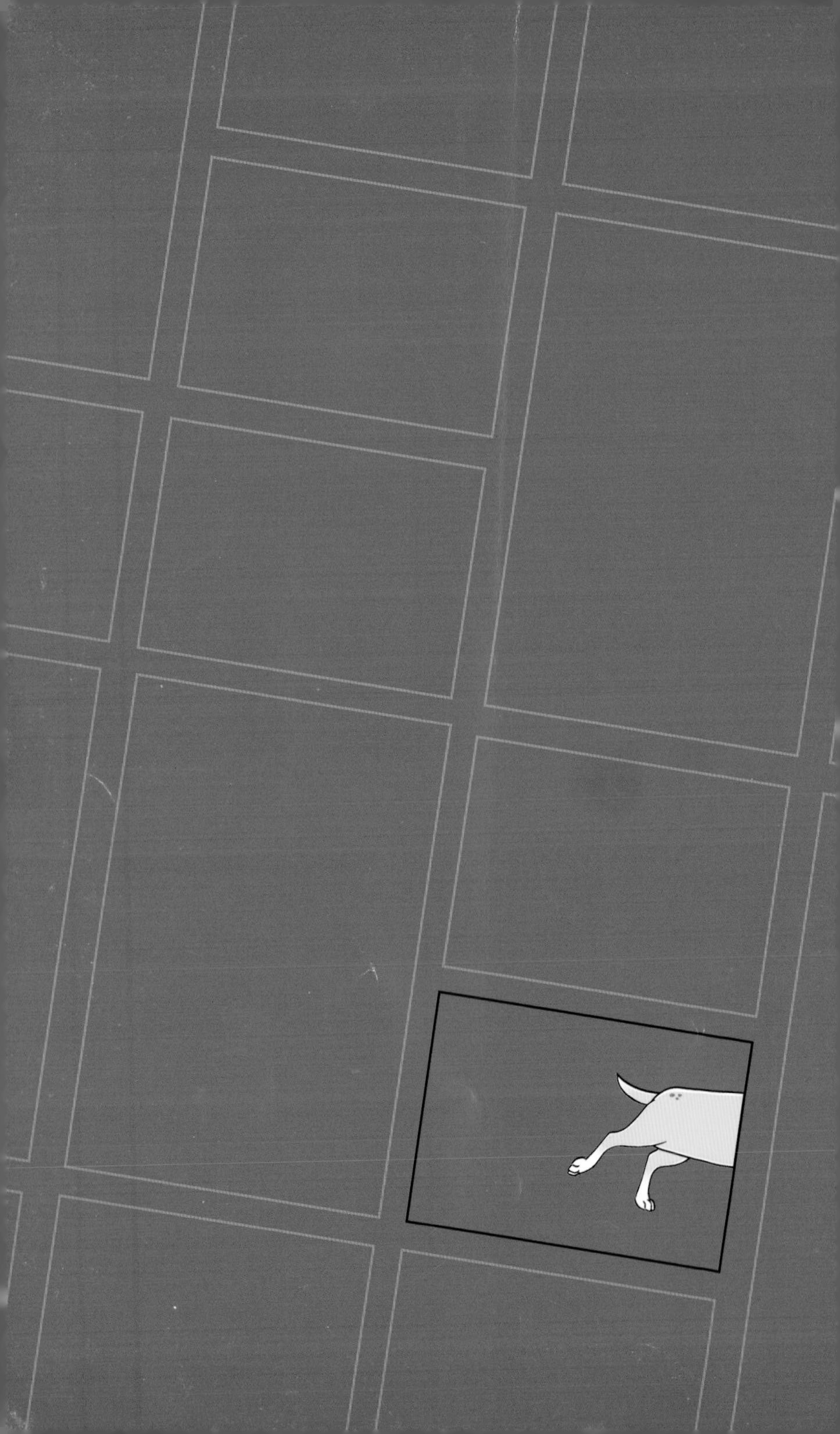